Serious

LESBIAN EROTIC
STORIES & POETRY

Pleasure

Edited by the Sheba Collective

CLEIS
PRESS

Published in the United States by Cleis Press Inc., P.O. Box 8933, Pittsburgh, Pennsylvania 15221, and P.O. Box 14684, San Francisco, California 94114.

Originally published in England by Sheba.

Printed in the United States.
Cover design: Ellen Toomey
Cover photograph: Jill Posener
Logo art: Juana Alicia

Library of Congress Cataloging-in-Publication Data

Serious pleasure : lesbian erotic stories and poetry / edited by the Sheba Collective.
  1st ed.
    p.   cm.
  ISBN: 0-939416-46-8 (cloth) : $24.95. — ISBN: 0-939416-45-X (paper) : $9.95
  1. Lesbians—Literary collections. 2. Women—Sexual behavior—Literary collections. 3. Lesbians' writings, American. 4. Lesbians' writings, English. 5. Erotic literature, American. 6. Erotic literature, English. I. Sheba Collective.
PS509.L47S47   1991   91-10930
810.8'0353—dc20   CIP

First Edition.
10 9 8 7 6 5 4 3 2 1
ISBN: 0-939416-46-8 cloth
ISBN: 0-939416-45-X paper

Grateful acknowledgment is made to the following for permission to reprint previously published material: "Living as a Lesbian Rambling," "Vicki and Daphne," "Great Expectations," "Sexual Preference," and "Nothing" by Cheryl Clark were first published in *Living as a Lesbian*, and are reprinted with the permission of Firebrand Books. "The Art of Poise" by Barbara Smith first appeared in *Gay Scotland*.

CONTENTS

INTRODUCTION

after the last bookstore was razed,
the faggot owner — once noted, now hunted
— smuggled me the latest in dyke fiction from
fiji.
i had to eat the manuscript before i
could finish it.

i was already underground, though,
that time my journal was nearly
seized in the middle of the night
by uniformed children, blondish,
forcing the door.
and one time in the middle of the afternoon
in a park, a mustachioed gent in trench coat,
no hat, balding, subpoenaed it.
(recognized me from a photograph in some
obscure literary review before my licence
was revoked. it was a stunning photograph.)
i outran him.
he yelled at me, shaking his fist:
    'hey, poeta, hope you have a good memory.
    memory is your only redemption.'
hell, i'm lucky.
i could be hiding some place where
they kidnap you.

torture you on metal tables.
break your fingers.
i could be never-heard-from-again.

a homeless mercenery tells me
'detention is like solitude. and don't poets
need solitude. they'll let you have a western
classic or two, a norton anthology.'
'hell, what about a spanish-english dictionary,'
i ask him as he pulls a leisure suit over his bush
fatigues.

(my reveries were confiscated years ago
but my obsessions do me just as well.
a lot harder to manage but sexier.)

around the time stevie wonder's songs were
banned in south africa, a harried editor looked up at
me from my manuscript, shaking his head, said:
'maybe in thirty years we can anthologize an
excerpt.'
(hell, i mimeographed the thing myself and
gave it out in the quarantine.)

but hell, i still don't know what it's like
to be blocked by bayonets and frisked for
the color purple or be forced to dance
around a bonfire while my favorite passage
from Pushkin burns before my eyes.

today an actor who hasn't had work
since they stopped casting lesbians
pointed out to me from a book not my own:
'this word can get you executed.'
i'd never written the word.
but it was a good word.
it called me.

i had to write it or it would write me.
the pages of my journal were all written up
with words censored years before
they stopped selling blank paper, pens,
ink.
a few people had monitors.
i sneaked back into an old safe house,
raided during the bombing of tripoli.
i loosened a brick and pulled out a suppressed
manuscript, a tasty little piece of interracial
erotica i'd written before the emergency.
i wrote the word over and over,
large and small,
in cursive and in roman, bold and fine
on the back of every sheet.
i wrote it with my left hand
as well as my right.
i recited it every time i wrote it
played with my sex as i wrote it
over and over
and said it as i came
over and over ...

　　'hey, poeta, memory is your only redemption.'

Living as a Lesbian Underground: futuristic fantasy ii
for Luisa Valenzuela
by Cheryl Clarke

Now more than ever before it is easier to imagine, indeed witness, our sexuality being driven 'underground'. In the last twenty years since the first days of lesbian and gay liberation and feminism we have become ever so slightly complacent about the danger under which we live our lives. With legislation being passed which not only restricts our access to public funds but induces a form of self-censorship which could endanger our future collective memory, we have no other option than to continue to write and record our lives and our passion as we know it. We do not intend to sink passively into obscurity and are optimistic enough to believe that there are thousands upon thousands of lesbians, gay men and our allies who believe this also. Our sexuality marks us as 'other' and in *Serious Pleasure* we celebrate that 'otherness' as a vital component of our life-force, without which we would not be.

Lesbians have been writing and reading books which speak to our lives for ages. There is a significant and growing body of literature which comes from and is about different lesbian experiences. There are books about relationships, coming out, daily life, lesbian psychology, theory, parenting, race, class, sexuality and many novels which take on the multifaceted character of our lives. But there is still a dearth of novels or stories which focus on lesbian sex as a thing in itself, the very force which drives our lives and our passion.

We decided to publish a book of lesbian erotica because, quite simply, we wanted to read it and we knew that we were not the only ones, a huge number of lesbians 'out there' wanted to read it too. Good girls, bad girls, in love or out, young or old, we wanted to read about lesbians making love, fucking, desiring other women, desiring themselves, making each other dizzy with lust, turning each other on, delighting each other beyond belief, taking each other to heaven and back, sometimes disappointing each other, having sex in their heads while sitting in meetings or on buses. We wanted to read about the possible and the impossible, the fantastic and the realistic, the imagined and the acted out, the simple and the complex.

We discussed this book for ages. We agreed that we all enjoyed reading arousing, sexy, hot stories about lesbians, but we argued over stories we had read (mainly from the USA) and what they did for us, and our opinions differed. Was the aim of a 'good' erotic story to explore a crucial dimension of lesbian identity in a revealing, yet sensitive way or was the to aim to titillate, turn on, lead to masturbation or making love with someone? Our discussions were endless. We did not reach a conclusion, but decided that the two aims could co-exist. Curling up with a well crafted, imaginative, innovative lesbian novel or short story which deals with sex can inform our identity as lesbians, and bring us to a new place in our creative lives. At the same time, it can move us sexually. Getting into a story whose primary aim is to arouse us sexually is neither wrong, nor necessarily separate from any other aim of fiction.

We do not expect every lesbian to like, approve of, or be driven to having sex by every story in this book. Some are about rough sex, some about soft and gentle encounters, some entertain fantasies which we yearn for and others we fear may become a reality. Some of us like both these facets in our sexual lives, others like one or the other, some may not like either, but how are we to know if such stories do not exist?

We see the collection as representing the diversity not only of our experiences and histories but of our desires and sexual practices. We do not label this approach as liberal; the differences within *Serious Pleasure* are framed by a feminist perspective which is informed by a radical approach to the politics of sex, race, class and culture. It is a perspective which celebrates the specificity of lesbian sexuality but does not see that sexuality as cut off from the rest of the world. We believe it is crucial for us to encompass all aspects of our sexual needs/desires, however contradictory they may seem to us, as well as all the other aspects of our lives which inform the very way in which we deal with the world and each other.

We are well aware of the ongoing and many leveled discussion and arguments about what constitutes the difference between erotica and pornography. What, if anything, is the difference between lesbian erotica or pornography and that written by heterosexuals or gay men? We feel that these debates are part of a wider discussion about representation, about the construction of lesbian sexuality, about sexual politics and sexual practice. They are fuelled by a need to find the perfect answer, the fine balance between political correctness and personal experience: a balance we are still searching for and may never find as a 'community', but may find within ourselves. We should not see those differences between us as dangerous or threatening. It is more how we express those differences and treat each other that needs to be considered: if we are to respect ourselves we must first respect each other.

We are confident about the 'rightness' of publishing this book. Sex between women can be an exciting, lustful, wonderful experience. We know that lesbian sexuality is still considered sick and peverse by much of the rest of society and that to write openly and in celebration of it, is to reveal ourselves to a powerful and largely unfriendly world. We know also that there are men out there who will get off on our 'perversity'. In a male-dominated world, lesbian sex is both a serious and disgusting affront to men's indispensibility and a rivetting turn on to some of them. Indeed, how long do we wait before we write about *all* our concerns and make them available to other women? At a certain point our confidence must override our fears. That is a risk we are willing to take as opposed to remaining silent.

In asking women to write for *Serious Pleasure*, we were asking for a great deal. Writing is always a risky business and even more so when writing about that most intimate of pleasures, sex. Yes, sex is political but it would be ridiculous not to acknowledge that while it is political it is also something which for most of us, most of the time, takes place away from the 'public eye', away from any notion of collective accountability, away from our friends and family. In other words there is nothing about sex itself that privileges it above the rest of life and makes it particularly 'natural' or separate from everything else we do, or above feminist scrutiny and criticism. But the question of how we make it political in a *real* way remains one of feminism's ongoing debates. How also do we deal with an area of life which so clearly draws in unknowns from the unconscious as well as presenting us with an already heady brew of body (beloved and hated), emotions (what is this thing called lust, let alone love?), and mind.

When we set about putting together *Serious Pleasure*, we wanted it to encompass the wide variety of our lives and our desires. We wanted our differences to be reflected in it — not only on the level of our histories and cultures, but also on the level of our erotic fictions. We wanted the list of writers in the book to represent at least a good many of the different realities we occupy in western English speaking countries. We have only succeeded partially in drawing this diversity together. We contacted a whole range of women to write for this collection, but there are absences. We see those absences not as failure, but as having very particular political reasons. The reality of life, not just here in Britain but internationally, is such that those under most pressure often feel they have to make quite stern decisions about political and practical priorities.

When we asked women, whose lives are already at risk in bleak Britain of the late 80s through racism, poverty, and heterosexism to write about lesbian sex, it is not surprising that some declined. It is not that sex is a luxury to such lesbians; it is more that other concerns must take precedence in their public/ political lives. On the other hand, some decided to wait and see if we could pull it off, or if they would even like what had been produced. One book could never seek to represent the entire cultural and political diversity of lesbian lives, indeed this is just the first intervention of its kind and must be seen in that context.

Serious Pleasure is in no way a lesbian sex manual. In the same way that fantasy is not an indication necessarily of what any individual will do in 'real life', neither are the stories in *Serious Pleasure* what either the authors or the readers necessarily 'do'. Safer sex is a case in point. Interestingly none of the stories submitted to

11

us included safer sex as an issue either to be addressed in the context of the story or built into a sexual encounter (except for a brief mention in 'Masturbation is for Wankers', Barbara Smith). Do lesbians in general still believe that AIDS is not a significant reality for them in terms of sexual transmission? We would guess that this is true and may be the primary reason for the absence of any mention of safer sex in these stories. For some who are concerned about the need for lesbians to be aware of safer sex between women, what exists in fiction, whether it is set out as a fantasy or as reality, is not necessarily what will happen when women have sex together. We believe that all lesbians should think long and hard about HIV and AIDS and seriously take on the hows and whys of safer sex. For some, erotic stories consciously built round safer sex practices might be helpful. *Serious Pleasure* has not included that possibility in its brief. Even if unprotected lesbian sex was clearly a high risk behaviour we do not believe that all fictional writing or visual representation of lesbian sex should immediately incorporate safer sex guide lines. However, we feel it is important that the issue of safer sex is always acknowledged in some way. We have included some information which you will find at the back of the book.

We have spent a good deal of time going through what and who is not in *Serious Pleasure*. In fact many women sent in stories and poems and wrote accompanying letters which left us in no doubt that this was a book long overdue. Not only does this book include contributions from previously published writers, but we are also proud to have included a number of excellent first time authors. Clearly this is indicative of the wealth of talent and creativity amongst lesbian writers today.

A lot of the stories are first and foremost about sexual encounters or fantasies of them. 'Doing it' or imagining 'doing it' are dominant themes, therefore only some of the stories and poems take an approach which is outside of what we have 'traditionally' come to think of as 'sexual'. There are few stories in the book which, although charged with eroticism, do not end in sex. No one can deny that this collection embraces a wide variety of challenging and stimulating styles and approaches.

It is our hope that *Serious Pleasure* will be the first of many books which attempts to capture those serious and pleasurable moments of our lives, minds and bodies that make us who we are. Ultimately, we hope this book gives pleasure and inspiration.

So, dear reader, enjoy ....

The Sheba Collective
London,
January 1989

SOME ORGASMS I'D LIKE TO MENTION

MARIA JASTRZEBSKA

In books which are extremely / few and far in between / that I've read / where it happens at all / most of the women are called Diana. Their slender (what else) fingers hold the stems of wine glasses /before moving / left, right, up around nipple,thigh, breast, back /left shoulder again / by which time I'm lost / while they reach (what else) one perfect orgasm / after another (all at first try) moaning.

Along with some small details
like having to go and pee
the doorbell ringing
your mother calling
the cat trying to join in
farting at the worst moment
even getting up for a drink of water
when your mouth is dry
let alone your period starting
what these books don't mention:
the orgasm which never arrives
leaving you confused and sore
annoyed but probably blaming yourself
the orgasm which trickles out
stops too soon
makes you cry
remembered pain

sheer loneliness
the orgasm which isn't that great
compared to
which you shouldn't do
other ones.

Even there / in lesbian books I've read, they didn't describe that
much / mostly the moaning or moistness / all those directions just
to confuse you. / Perhaps they don't want to kiss and tell, after all.
I don't really blame them. / These things are personal.

If it wasn't taboo
so fiercely denied everywhere
I don't know if I'd be mentioning
the luxury
along with the ordinariness of it
the orgasms which make you feel
I never
or I always knew
it could be
just like this
all the worrying
then suddenly not worrying
anymore at all
what the neighbours can hear
what will happen
the nothing can stop us now
look on her face.

THE TENNIS SKIRT

BERTA FREISTADT

It is summer and the school smells. It smells of all the usual things;
polish, stale food, sweat, unwashed hair, talcum powder. It also
smells of things more intangible like impatience, exam nerves, lost
registers and frustration. Although there is no sun in the grey
summer sky, we know it is summer by the sports uniforms. Hockey,
football and indoor athletics have been replaced by tennis and
cricket. Cricket for the boys. We are all wearing T-shirts, cotton
trousers and dresses. Even I have shaved my legs and wear a bra.
Classes are more difficult to control if nipples are displayed. Though
no such delicacy appears to concern Jacky. She is the beautiful games
teacher with whom I have been unrequitedly in love for six months
and whose splendid and disconcerting breasts are frequently
revealed in this warmer weather with the discardance of track suit
tops and cardigans.

Oh Jacky, never before did I admire so much the simple
white airtex shirt; well known are its properties for allowing the
pores to breathe but I am discovering its other qualities, how it clings
and moulds and reveals. Once more I avert my eyes and wonder
why she is allowed to stand in the middle of the staff room with
her arms and breasts raised, vulnerable and waiting under the guise
of taking off her sweater. I know she only does it to tease and one
day there will be an instant conversion to lesbianism by all the
women in the staff room when she will get knocked over in the
rush. This of course is a sad thought, for now that I force myself to

16

sit as far away from her as possible I will only be at the top of the pile and not deliciously at the bottom ... this is only one fantasy ... there is another. The tennis skirt fantasy.

The first time I saw it the tennis skirt was in her hands. It was a small piece of navy blue pleated material, possibly a child's. But the very next day she strode into the staff room in that friend of my dreams the white airtex shirt and the same navy blue frill round her own arse. I couldn't believe my eyes. I had to sit down, it had never occurred to me that it belonged to her. How did she ever control a class dressed up in that thing? My estimation of her as a teacher soared. She wore that garment all summer, no quarter. Briefly, I thought I was turning into a man; staring, obsessed, lecherous. I quickly pushed this from my already overheated mind, I had enough problems without inventing more. I wasn't a man and I wasn't objectifying her, I was admiring her in the long, old, respected tradition of lesbian adoration. Fantasy was as much a part of that tradition as was sending letters declaring your love and being speechless with embarrassment for months after.

She was of course completely unembarrassed about her appearance, or so she seemed. Personally, I thought she'd shortened the skirt to wind me up, there seemed no other explanation. You Jezebel, I thought, how can you dare. Supposing she sat next to me in that skirt, supposing I was wearing a dress, and supposing the bare flesh of her smooth golden leg touched mine, what should I do? For of course they were smooth and tanned and like the strong pillars of a temple. Oh, let me worship beneath that roof ... and the tennis skirt fantasy was born.

It went like this ... one touch of your divine legs and I would swoon to the floor before you. Would you close your eyes or would you watch me with a smile on your lips? I hope you would have your eyes open, at first, so you could see the smiling revenge in mine. We would look at each other, the goddess and the acolyte, invisible to the rest of them with their coffee and their mark books.

I would start at your ankles with a kiss, daring to touch at last, to hold and pretend that you loved me. I could feel the sweet curve of your calf on my cheek as I leant my face against you, dying a little death of relief. And in leaning, I must hold fast in order not to fall, and in holding, feel your strength and your power flow into me, giving me the courage to be bold. So I want to take rather than merely worship, to transform that kind smile on your lips to a gasp of shut-eyed ecstasy. So, there in the staff room while they are quarrelling about standards and fourth year discipline, I put my hands on your knees and ease them apart. I abandon my kisses and submit to an overwhelming desire to bite your thigh, there on the inside where it's softest and not so golden. Where only your most intimate, most darling love is permitted; and today, now, I am she. Your legs are stretched out straight either side of me and as I bite you, but gently, I will not leave a mark, I promise, as I bite you I hold on to those strong, long legs of yours as I would to a life raft in a rough sea. And bites become kisses once more, and my hands with their long fingers are at the top of your thighs under the pleated frill which ripples now in harmony with the waves of that sea. Higher, higher I strain and pull myself up further into the protecting roof of those pleats, my thumbs so near to lifting white elastic, my index fingers screaming with anticipation, with foreknowledge that what they will find, what they want, will be in such contrast to the smoothness, the coolness, the firmness that they have touched so far. They, I, melt and dribble with desire for all things hot and wet and wiry and above all, for you my so desired, my so beautiful woman.

By now she is so full of desire herself, and we are both making such a lot of noise that we are disturbing an important discussion on staffing levels, so I would take pity on us and transport us both to my bedroom with closed door and curtain and take all our clothes off, not before stamping up and down a little on that tennis skirt, but the bell goes and I'm due to face 3BW. Oh woe!

BOX S217

BERNADETTE HALPIN
for Gilly Green

Autumn might be the worst time of year to lack a lover. We were agreed on that, my best friend and I, as we sat in my kitchen one late Friday night and considered the prospect of the coming cold months. Our long-term lovers had left us for inferior women — we were agreed on that too — but as we pulled the rings on our third can of lager, this conviction gave us less comfort than it used to. However inferior these women, our exes were spending most of their sleeping and waking hours with them. We'd heard the word.

'So where do you want to go to tonight?' Clare quizzed me across the table; though we both knew we had only two bad choices: a huge metallic disco further north where the volume made your beer vibrate, or the cramped basement bar where my fags had been lifted in front of me by a woman who made me feel drunk to look at her.

'There's nowhere, is there?' I replied, 'I'm pissed off going out every weekend to get booze spilled over my best clothes and have some woman look at me like I'm a loony 'cause I ask her to dance. Remember last Friday?'

The weekend before we'd driven up to the metal hangar and stood nonchalant in a corner where the music hurt least.

'Anyone you fancy?' Clare had yelled into my ear, while I scanned the hundred or so women there with that same mix of willingness and despair that overcomes me when I have to choose from a dozen pair of jeans.

'Oh, I don't know ... I guess that woman in the white trousers is quite nice.'

I couldn't tell too much about her, except she was large and dark-haired (two things time has proved I like in a woman) and held her pint in a forceful kind of style that appealed, at least from thirty feet away.

'Ask her to dance!' Clare bawled again determined, I suppose, that one of us should make some moves that night.

'What — to this?' I shouted back. From the distant dance floor came amplified a noise, sister to that my hoover had made the morning before, dying in the middle of my front room carpet, while women danced like so many deckchairs. I glanced furtively at White Trousers. Were any of those women circled about her, her lover? or were they all mates too — out on the town and looking? Only one way to find out, and Clare's eyes were by now relentless.

'Would you like to dance sometime tonight to something?'

White Trousers turned to me; a young robust woman all in pale cottons, with eyes as dark and steady as her beer. And steadily they measured me: from my rolled-up jeans' ends to the neat space between my shirt buttons where I'd forced the iron's nose that afternoon, anxious I should look flawless on my Friday night out. But I must have missed something in all my preparations, because when her eyes reached mine again, she only said, without emotion,

'No, not really.'

'Oh, right, thanks.'

The thirty feet yawned, the lights offered no cover, and my legs moved badly out of time to the hoover, all the way back to Clare.

'Well?'

'Let's go home.'

'So I'm not going there or doing that again, not after the mess you got me into last time.' Clare looked back at me, her eyes unrepentant and amused above the mouth of her lager can.

'I vote we look through Lost In The City again.'

'Oh God, no!' Clare protested, 'There's nothing in there this week except 'femme looks for non-scene butch ...'

Each latest edition, she and I read through the catalogue of lonely hearts, stopping at the bold type that said LESBIAN or even GAY WOMAN, while both understanding we'd have no truck with a woman who hadn't got past 'gay'. I fished the magazine from out of the sofa cushions and spread its pages close between us. As usual, there were only a handful of ads from our girls.

'How 'bout this one?'

My finger drew Clare's eyes to 'ATTRACTIVE LESBIAN, 26; seeks friends for fun out, and maybe that special someone for cuddles in. Non-smoker, likes theatre, arts, therapy, and long walks.' Twenty-five words that threw what image into unknown readers' minds?

'Too young' said Clare rudely, 'and what does she mean 'into therapy and long walks'? She'd probably leap out of bed first light, Sunday mornings and want to hike across Hampstead Heath chatting about letting go of our mothers — and she doesn't smoke. Anyway, I want someone who's into a good fuck, not cuddles.'

She blew smoke in my direction to prove one of these objections.

'Clare!!'

Really, for a woman who was a social worker and grew up in Twickenham, she could be downright bawdy at times.

'Look, it's not so you only want a good fuck (my lips made the second word furry). You want someone who's caring and good for you, and not liable to do you over the way Helen did.'

Clare's eyes reflected blue, with an icy tableau of indifference and scorn.

'Okay, I'm sorry I mentioned Helen ... okay, we're after uninhibited sex, a good time, and no emotional hangovers.'

Twenty minutes later, the ads had yielded nothing more than outrage and dismissal.

'Why do some women write 'slim' — it's so down on other women ... and who cares if they're 'graduates' or 'professional'?'

Somehow it was comforting to know that, despite the years and the disintegration of our once separatist ideal, Clare and I could still breathe, smoke and seep lager over women who put other women down. I thought of my past lover and hers; not dissimilar women — addictive, volatile, arrogant and endearing. Women we'd bitched and cried over together when they were our lovers, and whom we still ached for, evenings like this, when every other dyke seemed as monochrome and dreary as the grey lines we read through.

'There's nothing for it,' I said finally, as the pages were closed and two more cans pulled open. 'We'll have to put in our own ads.'

'We can't do that!'

'Sure we can — why not?'

I went to my desk and came back with two sheets of paper and biros.

'Right!' I said, decisively as the late hour and lagers would allow. 'We've got twenty-five words to sell ourselves in.'

I lit another cigarette and bent my head to the paper. How to distill myself into twenty-five words? What said most about me? What did I remember women had ever got off on about me in the past? It was hard, trying to cross to that particular alien country. My hands, my eyes, my height, my humour? One woman still languished over my skinny wrists evenings we spent together — another had stayed with me for three years because she loved my 'sensitivity'. What did she mean? Anyway, I couldn't put 'sensitive' into the ad; other women might think I lived my life through my menstrual cycle or lay on sofas drinking herbal teas. Well, begin with the definites: age, star sign, and dyke; the last had all the connotations I wanted. Sagittarius, 34 ... shouldn't I say something of what I looked like, what I was into? Blankness loomed; there was no-one in the mirror, and I couldn't remember a damn thing about how I spent my time.

I looked across to Clare for inspiration, to find her biro had scrawled only angry whorls onto the paper, nothing more.

'I can't do this,' she answered my questioning look. 'There's nothing I can think to say. I'm so boring, and no-one will fancy me anyway.'

'Loads of women fancy you!'

'Who?'

'Well ...' I faltered, '... you're great. You're really giving and loyal and fun.'

She frowned; I'd begun to describe her like a woman who was into cuddles.

'And you've got a great body.'

That was true enough. I'd admired Clare's breasts and bum a score of times we'd slept over together. She looked pleadingly at me.

'Okay, I'll write it for you. But only if you'll write mine.'

That was how we came, my best friend and I, to interview the bereft but still hopeful selves of each other, and so translate into shorthand the romantic and carnal and downright slobby natures of each. That was how I came to be Box S217.And that was how I found myself, six weeks later, approaching the side door of a pub to meet a stranger who'd written from west London.

Of the fourteen replies that had come in staggered deliveries, hers had been the most promising: 40 years old, working class, and smart enough to string together three pages with wit and lucidity. I'd also lit upon a certain raunchiness there that caused me to clean out my ears and floss my teeth with particular care that evening. And to choose the most upfront of the three scents I had in stock. This might be a Paco Rabanne kind of night, I mused, as I touched it on around shoulders and throat. I'd chosen the pub because it was where the local lesbians hung out, and on Thursday nights had an 'older women's space' in the back bar. For over thirty-fives. But being with an older woman, I'd be allowed to tag along.

I spotted her the moment my toes touched the carpet inside the pub, sitting on a stool at the end of the curved bar and looking around to me as the door rattled closed. Light hair, pale eyes, a self-possessed smile.

'You must be Annie.' She extended a courteous hand.

'Yes. Caroline?'

'That's right — want a drink?'

I noticed she shared my taste in booze: Guinness standing a pint high and carrying a deep head of cream.

'Thanks, I'll have the same as you.'

My pint was pulled ('Hi Annie, how you doing?') and we moved to a cushioned corner beneath the fag machine.

'So what do you do?' I asked her, 'You didn't mention that in your letter.'

'Actually I teach Classics.'

Her voice was wrong. Even we girls educated out of council estates didn't talk like Radio 4 turned on at reggae volume. I yearned for a juke-box, and felt a sweat, born of anxiety, rise beneath the scent made for nights suddenly shorter than this promised to be. Classics? Wasn't that Rome and Greece — chariots plying through landscapes of sand, men in bathrobes bawling Latin under murderous suns? Caroline explained Classics at length to me; and to the men who'd taken their familiar stand between ashtrays and barcloths. The only interruptions were the several women who stopped at our table to greet me.

'Hi Annie, how are you?'

'Fine,' I hesitated, 'and this is Caroline.'

An hour later, Caroline and I were amongst the first in the queue for the darkened bar, curtained off, where older women could share what older women preferred. This revealed itself as a dozen round tables, clothed and candle-lit, a sound system issuing passé melodies from one corner, and a piano where a woman sat waiting to play. The hangar and its electronic migraine faded. This is nice, I thought, as we took a table behind the singer. Caroline was still buoyant and earnestly conversational, though rather flushed by now, I noticed. Was she drunk? I had experience of what three large Guinness and their whiskey hangers-on could do, but with strangers it was hard to plot the signs from charmingness to collapse. Her eyes were pale as fog now, but in the easeful atmosphere of soft flames and conversation I relaxed better than I had done under the scrutiny of curious acquaintances in the outside bar. Caroline smiled at me ecstatically.

'I'm having a great time — I like you a lot.'

'I like you too,' and meant it for the first time that evening.

She slipped an arm with almost studied friendliness behind my shoulders and left it there. A phrase from my advertisement — 'seeking another for passion/conversation' — flared behind my eyes like neon. Oh God. What had seemed bold and witty in my familiar kitchen now perhaps was promising a shared cab home to my bed to this woman drawing deep on her fourth pint and leaning ever closer to me. I couldn't even blame Clare.

Then the woman three feet from us began to sing. Her voice was sweet and light and tremulous, perfect for the Joni Mitchell classic she chose to open with: 'A Case of You'. I closed my eyes to savour better the aching lyrics I'd known by heart since leaving home. I didn't recall Joni had ever recorded the song as a duet; but now as I listened there was another voice too that knew all the words. Caroline's. Caroline was accompanying the song in her lecture hall alto, dipping her head earnestly in time like that ping pong blip I remembered would dance across the lines of songs learned when I was a child. During her set, the woman covered a dozen bedsit standards, each illuminating some solitary emotion. But if she ever became aware she was not alone, the singer didn't show it. Caroline never lost a line, and her phrasing by now was plucked deep from the well of her sinking glass. I wove my way through the copse of candles to order another pair of beers. There's getting drunk to forget — this was getting drunk not to know at all.

The sound system had usurped the singer by the time I returned, and the opening bars of some current love-song blared across the few feet of dance-floor: 'Lady in Red'. Jesus! did growing old mean believing this to be the height of passion? Apparently not, since nobody moved. Except Caroline.

'This is my favourite!' she gasped, 'you must dance!'

'I don't dance, I never dance,' I answered grimly. I wasn't wearing red, therefore I didn't have to dance, she couldn't possibly mistake me for anyone the singer was whinging on about. I clicked my seat-belt. I didn't move.

Caroline swayed in front of me, arms embracing some darling apparition, while her lips mouthed the words under water. The cigarette in her hand drew curves that would be me glowing in the half-light. Then it dived onto the floor. It was when I saw her knees almost buckle in her attempts to retrieve the lit end that I knew I had to take Caroline home.

My basement flat is only twenty sober minutes from the pub; that night it seemed we walked for hours. My arm tight around her shoulders held Caroline close and supported by me we crossed roads crab-wise, and I fought to remember I was the one who knew the way. We sang 'Lady in Red' in raucous duet — how did I come to know all the words? — while cruising the pumps on a garage forecourt. We struggled to light each other's cigarettes on a corner seemingly storm-tossed as an open boat. I drew deeply on mine and watched it glow against the backcloth of dark houses, a lighter sky. Caroline gestured gravely with hers toward a nearby bottle bank.

'Was this the face that launched a thousand ships, and burnt the topless towers of Ilium?' she declaimed.

A cab swept past indifferently, leaving us immobile in its wake. I stared at her — the question I'd been wanting to ask for hours suddenly voicing itself.

'You said in your letter you were working-class, so how come you talk like that?'

'Like what?'

'Like ...' Clumsy fingers seemed to grope my brain in darkness for the words, then turned over a child memory, '... like someone posh.'

'I learned to talk like this, to make myself understood. I'm from Yorkshire originally, but it didn't do — reading great literature in a voice from t'pits.'

She'd spoken the last words in flat northern tones, her pale face lit now with humour. Our eyes met, and for the first time that evening I recognised Caroline; the altered accent drawing back through years and guises I could understand. A memory surfaced from my own years of escape into books.

'When I was at college, one tutor called my accent 'Dickensian' — said nobody spoke like that anymore. Made me feel like a refugee from the underworld.'

'Well, I guess we both were, still are.'

We smiled conspiracy, mocking the pain that had driven us both through long transformations to the unlocated women we had become, owning another language.

It was a mild night, so rare in London we sat out in my tiny yard drinking oceans of tea. There was something tender in the smell from the ivy that scrambled haywire up the back of the tall house, something out of time, sitting there in the unfinished jigsaw of lights that fell from a dozen rooms above.

'Oh God! I guess I made a fool of myself in the pub.'

'No you didn't, you were fine.'

I recalled the note she'd hit during 'A Case of You' — 'I would still be on my feet, still be ooon myyy feet.' .... Even Joni had passed that one up. I giggled.

'They might want to hire you though, at the piano next week.'

We both exploded into laughter and clung together. The silence around was an invisible deep landscape; no sirens, no raised voices, no cats calling from the wall behind. It felt very good,

Caroline holding me; I didn't move away. She leant my head back and kissed me very long and deep. I wanted her; something in me drawn very far from another place in my life answering her warmth and familiarity. Caroline pulled back a little to search my eyes speculatively.

'Well, your ad did promise passion and conversation.'

'So it did,' I answered. 'Do you like talking in bed?'

We undressed each other though without a word. Her body stepping free of dark trousers, breasts falling loose from her shirt, was full and luminous, naked in a different candle-light. Beneath the covers I gave myself up to her arms, reckless against the desire I could feel hot along her skin. I pulled one leg high between mine, anchoring my need against her thigh, my tongue pushing past her lips deep into her mouth reaching for her. Leaning away for breath, I looked into eyes so pale I couldn't see their colour.

'You smell wonderful,' she said.

I thought of my own fingers against my throat where her mouth was now, touching perfume to my skin an age ago and wondering what the evening would bring. Somehow I didn't think Paco Rabanne was what she meant. Then when she plunged inside me, very soon and without being asked, I knew I was right, in what I'd read between the lines of her letter.

TRAPEZE

CAROLINE HALLIDAY

My tongue meets a rough raked valley small like rough grass or
is it ploughed earth   the taste is different   I wanted to put my
mouth   there but didn't dare   didn't know   how to move my body
down yours   gracefully and now you swing above me suppose we
were both on a trapeze/me below you and your body swinging
twisting as it does with a wildness   and I tie myself to your lipped
varied bushy tasting cunt not caring where the land is/ this is a
hillside ragged yellow flowers and even maybe thistles low down
hidden and delightfully prickly   who said donkeys were the only
ones

the nasturtiums stare   their stems cross-legged in the green
grass   their leaves like flat fat palms give me something reach me
look at my palm there's nothing   bare and clean/ their petals like
lobes of ears ears hung hanging weighty/ little bones in the ear
cartilage and their smell cuts across my face in a sweep like those
leaves down through sinuses up through sinuses brain eyes to smell
with orange-streaked transparent lobes of ears tongues reaching for
my lips to lick me softly   your tongue reaching wet and gentle and
playful

last night I put on that skirt found it recently black and
lovely material   cloth slippery and wet indented flowers raised
smooth and fitted all the way down curves of stomach nice isn't it
to know where your body is/ feel this is my skin boundary I know
who I am you can see me too

If you touch me womanlover in the hall or against the fridge
I would like that   if you put your hand up my skirt on the settee
I'll remember   I'll remember because my body does exist up here
under my skirt and I like your hand there

      sunday night is old lady's night I said joking/ when I get it

What does the rough talk mean what did biting
mean/nothing but fun   but I think it's touching the edges/ I've been
brought up on it touching the edges how can I explain that   taking
the edges into my life how could I not/ I've had years and years of
it what does it mean to us now   lesbians touching loving/ finding
our own ways unexpected I like feeling your desire unexpectedly/
incongruity could I say I like incongruity/asymetrical sex against the
fridge takes it away from sex inthebed/let's do it sensibly/ let's do it
suddenly when we weren't expecting it uncover my body decide/I
like to feel your decision/that's the cutting edge your power against
me the power of the river keeping to its banks   you can come and
look at her she'll touch you and you can go away you can wade in
her she'll be unaltered you'll be unaltered unless one is altered by
a dream a moment by the sea to feel the sand in your toes
waves cold crushing the feet's land   is one altered by a single look
at the sea I suppose so

      your hairs were lacy you'll phone in a minute

      secrets you reach my body
      secrets
      love is surely being able to stay with the secrets the
frightening ones and the lacy velvet edges the black silk skirt of the
soul raised flowers with the wide lacy sea drawing over it flowing
up a long way curved and wide/ and shiny wet sand as it slides
away   to touch the dry land of your soul oh the soul isn't dry/ but
maybe someone else's is when you need to reach it

      tearing paper leaves an edge is it soft or jagged? have you

ever thought about that   is it soft and beautiful or rough and untidy
        rough soft and untidy beautiful

    here's the passion here now I want to kiss you for a long
time slide inwards to a breath a beat of universes inside me this is
grey black air velvet sweetly clifflike over my face like your hands
covering my eyes as you kiss my mouth only
        are you there
        there is this great wave in me soft like cloth billowing you
can pass through it like cloud or the haze on a landscape or the way
the distance changes from a high place

        remember the bite of an olive
        the tight hard taste of the retsina
        the grit on your feet the gritty crystals of large and sand
white grit
        when I kiss you like this
        my mouth would swallow the universe my body drink you
all   watching the wave in you wanting them both together

    Yr hair is beautifully lively dark and crisp it hides and
covers glistens the edges of yr labia dark and velvet edged this is new
this is sunday evening this is a time for suddenness touch me —
you have plunged your tongue in my ear as we watch the rhinos
— they are heavy and roll on small hips and shoulders that continue
for ever right down to their heads horns   you plunge your
tongue/have you been watching me today

        when I lay down to rest I could see
        your body what I wanted
        the line of your buttocks I wanted my tongue
        to traverse like a cleft in mountain
        to touch all the soft places with my teeth the back of your
shoulders between your shoulder bones your neck soft against my
cheek jaw

to touch without interference to touch without any response
any responsibility for my own body except   what it wanted to do
to find the build up that I could find just whatever

to let you secret away anything you felt in you following
sweetly like a breath each nuance of arrival what would this mean
to be entirely yourself the other woman alone each alone and not
alone but separate   a line of dark velvet between   is this trust in
myself it would be   it would be difficult
if we take it slowly maybe there is something
if we take it slowly there is something different waiting
listen I want to come to you
I want to take you in the round circle of my arms hold you
all of you legs arms shoulders and feel your head your mouth you
want to reach me with your mouth suddenly
I want to come and hold you
and I am lying here
sleeping

I slide into you and it is not like before
you don't bite me anymore you say why is that

my fingers are all round you gliding on a smooth lip of skin
smooth as satin and smooth as warm water to plunge in

I lie close to you closer I am aware of my skin stopping
where I stop and the haze of me which blends closer closer inside
your breath your beat the skin I rest on
is it possible to know this moment closer
to go back/ on/ to be in that place where warmth touch food
sensuality were the smell of your   rise and fall of your/ denseness
of your close body in the moment before disruption

is it possible for the breath in me to meet at your lip to
meet at your mouth along the line of our bodies to meet below the
breath that sighs up softly from below rising and falling/ to find

your mouth there is a still peacefulness/ there is a still peacefulness
that says we meet   we meet here now

　　　　I slide my fingers on tracks as smooth as gleaming oiled
metal railways tracks in the light polished   This is underneath this
is underneath this is the other part of your mouth I find a
place through

　　　　　　there is an opening you want me to go to my fingers
　　　　　　meet here
　　　　　　it is not like
　　　　　　plunging
　　　　　　it is like warm earth over your head a cave comfortable a
tent with rugs and cloth and roof
　　　　　　a cave with jewel and sparkle food couches cushions
　　　　　　earthy
　　　　　　like walking in a forest green with light dripping/sun
shaking between leaves
　　　　　　a cave of bracken smell against my face green lacy fronds
like a shadow pressing my skin
　　　　　　meet here
　　　　　　to go in
　　　　　　there is green lava   there is earth rich and crumbly
　　　　　　to go in
　　　　　　is
　　　　　　I can explore here this is pleasure
　　　　　　you say I don't bite you anymore
　　　　　　there will be time for that
　　　　　　when the next round of
　　　　　　merging
　　　　　　meeting
skin
begins

34

HEALING

MANDY DEE

You could not heal me tomorrow
You must be gentle now
as I lie, softened and feeble;
horizontal — curled around
Your thigh
Lest sudden sleeping
Should force me into another discordant night.
Pervasive, ancient life-delight —
Should I spend my strength today?
If I take heart-healing from your eyes
and return soft loving with my lips
Could you hold me tomorrow
When confusion and shaking take me?
Are my hands resting on your cheeks tonight
Worth the next days draining of my life?
Years I have been weakening here:
the moment of my wanting passes —
My life passes,
I'd have life
If I could have life
Understand I'd seize at life and love
and You.
Desperate for life's-breath
I'd kiss you
And kiss you.

In lusty despair,
I am become a vampire
Seeking air,
Seeking air.
See how desire and disease divide us
Dear Heart, Shall we be Survivors
outliving these tearing fears?
If we must be chaste
Know that I love you
And kiss me gently
Hold me Here.

SHY — FRAGMENTS

MANDY DEE

In terms of Dr Martens
or karate
we can mention legs,
but you shy away:

and are shy
when the words
   inner thigh
are linked with lips

Mentioning women warmed in bed
you think of sapphic sunsets
and private declarations.
Warm bed, warm woman
I kiss you chastely, so tastefully
that our kisses might seem sisterly
without our lesbian symbols
woven into each nightdress
laughing,
so safe,
yes relaxing
warmed
In bed
I am softened
but still hunting.
I want no more old coy quotes

about undivided nights.
I am softened
loosened
open,
but breathing for your hands
I want this -
the explicit gentleness of fingers tips
I want us together
And your eyes could cloud over deep
deep; but not with dreams.
Will we feel and sense the shyness
the breaking open of our selves
our feeling
fear
hunger-healing
opening and opening

and deep, I want to trace the contours of your body
and deep, I want to taste the colours of your skin.

I COULD TELL

PEARLIE McNEILL

I saw her on the beach. She was strong-limbed and strode along with a jaunty air. It was sunset. I watched the huge golden shape slip down to the water. Slowly, it dropped from view leaving streaks of purple stained sky. When I drew my attention back to the sand and the softly curling waves I saw the woman again.

She was much closer now.

I watched as she made her way over two prominent rocks in the middle of the beach then she turned away from the water, though with the tide coming in as it was, there was lots of frothy foam to walk through. The water was so soft-looking I couldn't help thinking that it was like a caress on her bare feet.

I was sitting nearer to the promenade steps, my eyes intent on the woman's movements, my belly registering flutters of excitement. She came closer until, at last, there she was, standing right in front of me. I could hardly breathe. I didn't look up but kept my eyes fixed on an area of brightly coloured skirt, somewhere about her midriff height. Without a word she eased herself onto the rock positioning her body quite close to me. I kept my head perfectly still but the hairs on my arms seemed, suddenly, alive and crackling. I was convinced I must be leaning sideways as though responding to some strong magnetic pull.

It was then that I heard the ice-cream bell. She must have heard it too. She stood up and walked away.

I wanted to shout and plead with her not to go but instead I sat there, silent, unmoving, staring at the sea.

She was back in a minute or two, an ice-cream cone in each hand.

Now, at last, I managed to turn and face her. I could not take my eyes off her tongue and mouth as she devoured that ice-cream. Passion-fruit, I think it was.

I took the cone she handed me, ran the tip of my tongue around the outer rim, catching the cool drips that threatened to fall. By this time she was nibbling the edges of her cone. I could see her teeth, they were very even with a largish gap between the top two in the front. They must be strong teeth I decided, as I watched her taking small bites, the small movements co-ordinating well with the action of her hand as she turned the cone around.

A shiver of excitement rushed down my spine, spreading across my backside and then continuing on into my thighs.

Could she tell?

What if she left now?

What would I do?

The last of her cone had gone and she was carefully wiping her hands on a handkerchief she had pulled from her shorts' pocket. I hastily finished what was left of my ice-cream, then rubbed my hands back and forth across the seat of my shorts feeling uncertain as to what might happen next.

She held out her hand. I gave her mine and followed as she led the way towards town. Her flat was but a short distance from the beach.

We walked through the front door into a largish room. I don't remember much about it, except that there were piles of books all over the floor. I hurriedly searched for titles that might give me a clue but it was difficult to position my head at such an odd angle and the woman still had hold of my hand. She smiled at me briefly before making a path around the books and into another smaller room off the kitchen.

We were now in the bedroom. There were lots of plants and the walls were a sunny yellow. I noticed an old washstand, thick green towels and a floor of cork tiles.

I waited.

She began with my shirt buttons. I wanted to help her but I didn't. The stirring between my legs was urgent. I could feel myself swaying towards her, wanting to be touched, wanting to touch her, everywhere. She eased my shirt away from my shoulders, dropping it behind her. Next, she unzipped my shorts. I felt a wave of relief in remembering that I had worn my best pair and not my other, older ones, which had to be pinned halfway up the zip. Her very nearness was quite intoxicating. I could feel the urgency between my legs like an ache. I was in such a held-breath state it was as if my body might fall apart if I breathed too often or too fast.

I stepped out of my shorts. My skin was bare now. Dampness was coming from every pore. It was the skin on her neck that beckoned me, smooth and silky. She's an Amazon I thought. I was an Amazon too. With slow and deliberate movements I unbuttoned her shirt, unzipped her shorts and held her with one arm as I gently pushed the clothing down off her limbs.

We stood together under the shower. The water was tepid. It fell on our heads, our shoulders and ran in rivulets down the length of our mingled bodies. I moved even closer. She shifted her arms a little to make room for me. Our bodies fitted together beautifully.

We started to caress, to explore. Her hands moved all over me, seeking out, fondling, touching, kissing, nibbling, stroking. Oh, what lovely hands she had, they ran over my body as though familiar with every part of me. She seemed to know instinctively the things I liked. I stood in silent ecstasy as she sought out the places where I love to be touched.

Then it was my turn. I looked around for the soap. It was one of those quick lathering soaps and I turned it over and over between my hands until the bar of soap became too slippery to hold onto. I stuck the soap back onto the side of the bath and moved my hands slowly over the woman's body, beginning with her feet and moving upwards in slow, circular movements. Turning her with my hands on her shoulders, I rubbed more soap onto her back, beginning this time with her neck and working downwards, stopping here and there as the excitement ebbed and flowed between us.

A long time seemed to pass under that shower.

My mind was filled with images of pounding waves, gritty sand caught between toes, foaming surf, ice-cream licked by moist, pink tongues, cones nibbled by strong even teeth, bare flesh and warm breath, cascading water and groans of pleasure and delight. Once or twice I worried about the size of her next electricity bill but as she didn't seem to be giving it any thought, I tried not to as well.

At last I stepped onto the bathmat, wary that my unsteady legs might not be able to hold my weight. Her eyes followed me, a pleased expression on her face. I dressed and then hung the damp, green towel over the other end of the bath.

At the doorway, I turned back to grin at her, a big wide grin, full of warmth and appreciation. She grinned back and waved. The water was still falling over her shoulders. I walked out of the bathroom, through the outer room and then out of her flat. As I made my way home I looked up at the sky. It was quite dark. There were lots of bright stars up there, pushing and nudging their beauty through the velvety blackness.

It was going to be another fine day tomorrow.

WANDERLUST

STORME WEBBER

so yes, she said to herself, as her mind roamed again to the steamier
        places
she'd been missing/ cdn't help these vague & defined feelings of
        lust in so
dry a season. memories stayed fresh tho distant/ their heat having
        left
an imprint/ & touch as of late having been too confusing, too
        complicated, too .
none of the shit was ever running on the same track she thought,
head, heart, flesh & spirit all flyin off their own ways to wherever.
        but
who cd imagine a life that renounces love? who wd want to? not i.
in between touching (that tactile reminder of humaness, existence on
earth) we got to coast through findin inspiration in life's living, art,
our love for others known and not, and ourselves. all in all it's a
        blessing
to be living. it's just that sometimes, you need a little companionship
        within
that blessing. these were her preoccupations as she readied herself
        for
a night out. never daring consciously to summon a bevy of
        prospective
soft-eyed young women/ so just lookin for a few moments of body
freedom some pumpin music hopefully (she hoped the dj wd be
        on the

manic instead of depressive side of her strong personality).
the moon shone a deep-aged ivory, a peaceful but stirring roundness
over the city. as usual she wished she were actually flying around
somewhere in the astral with some particular deep eyed one/ two
warm hands clasping steady. this fantasy threatened to remove her
spirit from the dregs of 16th & valencia/ a medium small intersection
that was trying as usual to be bad. anyway it's a well known fact you
shouldn't hang around in no crossroads location without a
            destination
clearly in mind. the wrong idea might just snatch you up & then who
knows where you'd be. this thought brought her awareness back to
earth or should i say concrete level. yes, street, there you are again.
sometimes, usually late at night or maybe in the morning, before the
workday rush, there was a certain kind of city peace/ all those
            energies
at rest/ in the night mode, night feels more feminine. but tonight was
in full swing and a nervous erratic energy swirled through the street.

AMBIVALENCE

TINA BAYS

I was faced with having to make a choice. I didn't want to. I wanted, well, who knows what. That ambivalent desire to have no choice but to be overcome, not in control. A state I might yearn for in imagination but rebel against in practice. If, of course, I got the chance. Anyway it gripped me; I was head over heels in desire. Nothing was spoken. I read my fantasies onto her. She looked like my desires.

We met at social occasions from time to time and the peripheries of our political lives as lesbians intersected provocatively. Between times, I built my treasure house of fantasies. I didn't know her.

During that summer, away from cool days and colder nights of England, I slept by myself in a hot corner room in a house by the sea. Late at night, lying in bed, I would luxuriate in the heat, in my aloneness, in the muffled sound of the fog horn. I loved being there with the sea smells and sounds insinuating themselves into the hot, slightly claustrophobic room. No breeze those nights to stir the faded curtains or disturb the rising smoke from my cigarettes.

I would find myself thinking of her. An image, a feeling, merging into a fantasy. I was never aware until too late of what was happening. She made me do things; the confidence and certainty in her look, her voice, her actions allowed no compromises. And oh, how she wanted me! Any uncertainties about my desirability (and believe me, I had them) were reduced to trivia in the face of that desire. How my wetness was witness to the power of my fantasies.

It bemused me. I wasn't obsessed. I interacted as usual with friends and family, read, enjoyed food, went swimming and generally relaxed. But slowly in the summer evenings, alone, I filled my treasure house.

Gray, green London — home, away forever from home. Country girl in love with the city. I settle back into the familiar, back in the life. By contrived chance our lives begin to intersect again and much to my delight and terror there seems to be a different note of recognition in her eyes. Is something going on? I'm nervous of imagining that she really might have feelings for me. What if I'm wrong? What do I do about this? What might happen in a transfer from fantasy to reality?

Weeks later, walking together after a birthday meal for a mutual friend, it feels like a never ending ritual dance. I feel attuned to her essence — me who sneers at any notion of essences. I brush aside a voice of warning. Too late; I slide in and out of physical encounters even though we never touch. The space divides and yet connects me to her. I'm almost breathless with sexual longing and tension. Surely it takes two to generate this much feeling. I want it this way forever. I want to make love without touching. I'm dying to touch. I want to back off, forget it, forget it. I want to stop her in her tracks, reach out, slowly draw her head to mine and stand there, forever, breathing her in. The ambivalence delights and frustrates me. In fact I'm already set on breaking it down. I may regret my impatience.

What patterns are being enacted here? What predictable patterns played out? I want to understand *and* to be out of control — irreconcilable. My gut heaves, my cunt is alive. I'm soaking wet, I'm dazed. I want my breasts touched, my nipples teased, then hard, harder, please harder, bite me, bite me. I want to kiss, brush her lips, trace her face, dive my fingers into her hair, run them from the crown back, then pull slowly out through thick, dark tangled curls.

I hear her voice talking as we walk. I nod, hmmm, but I'm off and away, out of control and nobody knows. I want to push her into a deep doorway, kiss her throat as I hold her head against the solid wood, slowly and with pressure run my fingers between her breasts, in turn stroke up and brush each nipple tracing circles, pulling out, then greedy cup hard, and still hold her pinned to the dark door as cars and people pass us by. I want to put her against that door, sink to my knees in front of her, magically manoeuver her smart butch trousers down, eat her through her knickers, then hold onto her hips and pull the cloth down until she's naked from the waist to where her clothing entangles and holds her ankles. I want to tongue the soft skin of her thighs, deliberately run a line with my fingers right down her middle from belly to the top of springy, soft pubic hair, on to tease her clit and continue to the radiating heat and wetness of her cunt.

I want to force her legs apart, knowing she can't move far, open her lips, pull her towards my mouth. I want to hear her moaning for it, before I taste her, hungry with my tongue, tease round her cunt, run my fingers in circles around it, until finally, pulling her towards me with one hand holding her lovely arse, I enter her slowly as she cries out,

'Yes, more!'

Then me on my knees fucking her, licking and sucking her with passion and skill, my own cunt opening and burning, until she buckles with orgasm, stifling her cries for fear we'll be seen.

All this and we're still walking. How am I walking? In real life, late at night on a seedy street in London, I'm on the verge of coming. The object of my desire, whose fantasy fuck has left me wet and longing, stops to make a point. This real and flawed object has caught me miles away. Should I take her hand? I'm blushing;

does she feel it? Jesus, does she guess? Now there's silence and I feel as if all sorts of sexual words and sounds are going to force their way into articulation. God, this must be so obvious to her. How could I feel such a current if it's not reciprocated? Do I really want reciprocation?

My lips are sealed. We walk on, refer to the burdens of work, say our goodbyes, and part at the tube to head off in different directions. Is this a courtship? Her separateness excites me. It's what attracts me and I embroider impossible desires onto her. I'm waiting for her to make a move. I don't know her.

WHITE FLOWERS

JEWELLE GOMEZ

Louise picked up the ringing telephone absent-mindedly while she signed the shipping invoice. 'Sportswear on Four', she said. The moment of silence on the other end made her catch her breath and wave her co-worker away.

'May I help you?' she said crisply, knowing what the response would be.

'Yes, white flower, you can.' Then silence.

'When?' Louise asked in a dry, even voice although her heart raced. Her nylons began to feel scratchy on her legs; her skin prickled with excitement.

'Tuesday.'

Louise smiled. I guess Belmont Park is still closed on Tuesdays, she thought. She almost laughed out loud remembering how it had been when they first met. Each was eager to throw herself into the affair but then both were preoccupied with their own lives. Between swimming, yoga, volunteer night, working late, department meetings and, of course, the race track. There had been little time to have even a first date. Tuesday always turned out to be the best bet.

'Yes,' Louise said aloud. 'Tuesday, 6.30. I'll come up.'

That gave them twelve hours.

'Good,' came the throaty response. It was deep, musky and hard on the edges, like the voice of a teacher. Which it was. 'It's been a long time. I'll see you then.' Click. Her last words had been a bit softer.

Louise hung up the telephone. Her palms were sweating; her tailored blouse stuck to her back, in spite of the cool air circulating from the department store air conditioning system. The white carnation, signifying her position as a buyer, was crisp in her lapel. She held onto the desk and tried to catch her breath. It had been four months since the last time; she could make it until Tuesday, surely. Yet every part of her cried out, 'Now!' A saleswoman broke into Louise's disguised hysteria,

'Lou, this guy is driving me nuts. He insists ...'

'It's okay, I'll talk to him,' she answered with a smile at the red-haired girl who looked relieved. Louise knew how everyone hated to get involved in prolonged disagreements with customers just before closing time, particularly on a Saturday night. Louise needed any distraction from the wave of excitement which threatened to envelope her. She ran her coffee coloured fingers through her short, curly Afro and went out onto the sales floor.

Later she changed shoes in the stockroom and said good night to the women remaining behind to empty the cash from the registers. Without thinking she took the downtown train determined to avoid going home until as late as possible. That would mean one more night had passed, bringing her closer to Tuesday. She came up out of the subway relieved to feel the cool air in the square; crossed against the traffic, anxious to be inside the refuge of the Bar and with women again. Louise didn't glance around her until she was served her gin and tonic. Then she leaned back in her seat at the bar and listened to the music from the juke box with her eyes closed. She was plotting how she would occupy her Sunday and her Monday evenings when she felt a hand on her thigh. She opened her eyes slowly.

'Damn! I could'a had all your stuff and gone, slow as you are!' Then came a booming laugh from the large woman whose perfectly manicured, plump hand squeezed Louise's leg. They threw their arms around each other and laughed. Louise was happy to see her old friend Donna. 'I thought you'd be on vacation.'

'Naw, this year I'm going away in August, like the shrinks.' Donna said. Her barrelling laughter made her light brown curls shake all around her head and her blue eyes sparkled.

Donna and Louise almost always ran into each other unexpectedly and ended up spending the evening doing the town. Louise couldn't believe her good luck that Donna would turn up just when she needed her most. They ordered another drink for Louise and club soda for Donna — who'd been on the wagon for three years.

'Congratulations!' Louise said, toasting Donna with her glass.

When the woman next to Louise moved Donna climbed into the chair. She was a large woman, tall and broad. Built like a prison matron she sometimes said with a leer. That was an incongruous image beside the delicate whiteness of her skin and the passionate curl of her mouth. Louise, who was not a small woman herself, always felt comfortable with Donna.

They drank a little, danced a lot, then Donna drove Louise home. They sat over cups of coffee, almost silent for ten minutes when finally Louise began to talk.

'It's been like this for two years. Annie and I can't have a relationship. We've tried and it makes us both crazy. It's too consuming, emotional, too everything. But when we try to stay apart we feel like something died inside. I never know when she'll call. I don't even know when I'll write to her. We manage to keep it infrequent, but isn't it crazy?' She plucked the wilted carnation from her lapel and tossed it to the table.

'Hell, I wish somebody felt that way about me! If it's that good every four months or four years, who cares, go for it!' Donna said.

'Why don't we?' Louise said, as she stood and pulled Donna behind her into the bedroom. After all, they were good friends.

◆ ◆ ◆

Sunday filled itself. Donna left by noon then came laundry, paperwork, swimming, a call home to her grandmother. Louise mopped the floor, pressed clothes and decided what to wear for the rest of the week, beginning and ending with Tuesday. She played with her cat then rented two movies which she watched back-to-back, only pausing to prepare dinner.

On Monday, Louise arrived at the store early. She looked over the new shipment of jackets in the stockroom, made up marking instructions before most of the floor personnel had arrived then went upstairs to the cafeteria for coffee. She had only one cup. The muscles across her shoulders already felt as taut as guitar strings and it was too long a day for burn out. She vowed to have something soothing for dinner. Like a martini. Monday night Louise went to the gym then watched television and read simultaneously. After the eleven o'clock news was over she fell asleep easily, her final thoughts were of what was to come.

On Tuesday, she rose early, to give herself time to be sure she was satisfied with the rough cotton pants and bright blouse she'd chosen to wear. She peered at herself in the full length mirror in her tiny bathroom and was pleased. Her brown skin had a soft sheen under the coconut oil. Her large breasts and broad arse looked inviting in the rich material. She looked like a businesswoman. She looked like a woman who meant business. She slipped a vial of gardenia oil into her purse.

It turned out to be the kind of day that left everyone frazzled: an overflow of irate customers, a shortage of staff, an excess of snippy managers, all on a sale day. Louise maintained a small smile through it all. Her clothes remained crisp; her feet didn't even hurt.

When she emerged from the employees' ladies room at 5.30 pm her make-up was light and perfect. She looked as fresh as she had in the morning. More so. She walked to the Sixth Avenue bus. All the way uptown she concentrated on the crowded street and varied faces. She loved that about New York City: so many different kinds of people, all different colours, sizes, styles, beliefs all bumping together. The randomness of their union made her feel good. Louise got off the bus on Riverside Drive. At precisely 6.30 pm she rang Annie's doorbell and strode toward the elevator.

Upstairs, on the fourteenth floor, Annie jetted about her apartment. She plumped pillows on the couch and ran her fingers over the edge of the bookshelves although she was certain they would probably not even make it into the livingroom much less examine her library. Her body began to chafe in her clothes as it succumbed to the ache she felt for the woman ascending in her elevator. Annie opened the apartment door and they were both struck by a sudden shyness.

Annie's smile was brilliant. Her white teeth glistened, her dark skin was smooth as velvet. The sharply angled cut of her natural made her appear tall as she stepped back from the door and Louise entered. Annie wore white jeans, snug across her full thighs and a large man-tailored shirt which swirled in a teasing way around her broad shoulders and small breasts. Only a slight trembling of her lips revealed her excitement.

They watched each other for a moment as if to be sure nothing had changed in the past four months. Then Annie pulled Louise into her arms kissing her neck and cheek. She considered the tray of snacks she'd left in the refrigerator but could not stop herself from pressing Louise back against the closet door. Her body pushed forward, her leg moved between Louise's as if it could enter her. The smell of coconut oil and gardenias filled the air. She grabbed Louise's soft hair and pulled her head back. She stuck her tongue deep into Louise's mouth, unable to think of anything except taking her. The world dropped away from them. Louise arched her back from the hard wood of the door to press more closely to this woman who could fill her. She felt her hips moving in tight rhythm against Annie's leg and the demanding pulse of Annie's body possessed her. She came softly, unable to stop herself. They both laughed.

Annie asked, 'Would you like a shower? I'd meant to say that first.'

She watched as Louise took off her clothes and stepped into the steamy stream of water. She sat on the toilet seat watching Louise lather the soap. The tight bubbles slipped around the deep curve of her arse and turned in on her thigh.

Annie reached in to catch the next spray of suds as they glistened on Louise's belly. Her touch made Louise hasten. She rinsed the soap off and waited. Annie sat silently, gazing at Louise's body for as long as she could. She took in the heavy breasts and brown nipples, the plump arms, the thick hair which curled around Louise's cunt and the enticing curve of her calf. She tried to feel the texture of Louise's skin by simply looking it over. It made her breath quicken.

Louise did not fidget but stared ahead, feeling Annie's gaze as it slid over her skin. Annie then draped a thick towel around Louise's shoulders and rubbed her back, her arse, neck and feet: every part, roughly, lovingly. She then led Louise into the bedroom.

The blond wood of the bed stood out starkly against the dark blue and red African cloth that covered it. As usual the large vase on the dresser was thick with white carnations. Annie and Louise lay cross-wise on the bed, as if thrown down to catch their breath. Annie sat up on her arm to look again at this woman she could not live with and could not live without. They stayed that way for a while before Louise said, 'Okay, what's the news? Don't leave me hanging. Did you get it or what?'

They picked up their conversation as if it had been four hours since they'd been together not four months. Yes, Annie had bought her parents a VCR for their anniversary. The troublesome guy had dropped out of the Spanish class she taught. She'd just finished reading Audre Lorde's new book. Yes, she'd seen Louise at the Cinnamon Disco. That was the hardest part: not speaking when they ran into each other in public. Usually one of them would leave the bar, event or party, dragging along a puzzled companion.

Louise was up to twenty laps and yoga twice a week. She'd made new curtains for her bedroom, helped to organize the demonstration at City Hall and had seen almost every movie Annie had. Annie covered Louise's mouth with her own. They folded their bodies together like fitting parts from a pattern. Annie pulled away and caught her breath. Louise moved her hands from behind her head and started to caress Annie. But Annie caught her two hands and held them back at the edge of the bed. She clutched the two wrists in one hand and ground her hips into Louise. The soft moans coming from both of them rose to the ceiling.

'Please, please,' Louise almost sobbed.

Annie pushed against Louise's thigh, the roughness of her jeans bruised Louise's skin. She rubbed until she almost came but then stopped, pulled back still clasping Louise's wrists. Louise opened her legs and Annie finally entered her. She thrust her fingers inside deeply, filling the hungry heat that Louise offered. The thrusts began at Louise's clit, massaging it into madness then shot deep inside her convulsing womb.

Both women were telescoped lives. Everything they had ever been, would ever be, was condensed into these moments of passion. They lived only in this moment of complete submission to the desire that claimed them both. Annie's fingers seemed to elongate as she moved slowly in and out of Louise's cunt. The motion counterpointed Louise's shallow, quick breaths. She licked Louise's mouth and face, then her breasts. She moved on the left breast, licking around it, then across the nipple, dark against the sepia skin. She clamped her teeth onto it, sucking insistently. Louise thrust her hips forward trying to take in more. She could not really speak but 'please' hung in the air like the refrain of a rhythm and blues song as she expelled each breath.

'Oh yes,' Annie said, as if she too could bear it no longer.

She returned to Louise's mouth and grabbed her wrists again, stretching them out above her head.

'Oh yes!' she said, as she ploughed her fingers deep inside.

They both screamed with joy. Annie could not stop thrusting even as Louise came. Again Annie pushed inside, taking that long trail from clit to womb, harder and harder until Louise clamped her teeth shut, to stop the shout that arrived with her next orgasm.

They lay still, drifting into a light sleep for a few minutes. Then Annie got up slowly. Louise pulled herself up to the top of the bed and arranged the pillows under her head.

'I better feed you, or you'll complain that I'm a harsh mistress!'

She smiled as she stepped out of her white jeans and disappeared out the bedroom door. Her voice sounded as prim and hushed as a librarian's. There was a formality about her that seemed more intimate than her nakedness.

She returned with a tray of snacks and a bottle of Perrier Jouet. They nibbled on pieces of curried chicken, made from Annie's special recipe, while they talked, this time about movies and local gossip. They laughed a lot then fell silent. 'I think I'll always be yours,' Louise said.

She touched Annie's mouth with the tip of her finger, smearing the oil caught in the corners. Removing the tray from the bed to the floor, she climbed on top of her, tugging at the buttons of the large cotton shirt. She nuzzled Annie's small breasts through the yielding material. Louise didn't understand how it was possible to hunger for and demand domination with the same intensity as her need to take this woman from above. She was as sure a mistress as she was a subject. The staccato thrusts of Annie's hips sought out the touch that would bring her to completion. Could such a mutual desire exist? Is that why they could not manage except in this furious but circumscribed way? Louise did not think of that now. She had no thought, only her body's need, her hunger for the feel and taste of Annie.

Their eyes widened in surprise at the enormity of their desire. Louise slipped downward sucking every point of Annie's skin: breast, hip, navel until she licked slyly on the hair which covered the mound. She opened the lips of Annie's cunt gently before pulling the swollen clit into her mouth. Annie's gasp was sharp and Louise backed away, licking Annie's thighs and the small space between thigh and cunt lip. She licked playfully at the brown skin, inhaling the smell of a perfume she could never identify. Then she moved back. Annie made small crying sounds as if she were a child being punished. Her legs opened wider, still the soft flesh of her inner thighs brushed Louise's face, driving her further into desire. Her tongue whipped over Annie's clit, hungrily. They could no more stop this moment than they could stop the ocean tides.

Louise reached above and felt Annie's hands clutching the sheet. She pulled at Annie's wrists drawing her cunt down harder onto her mouth. She held her there while she moved in and out, sucking, breathing in the fire. She held Annie's clit full in her mouth as Annie screamed and strained against her until she was drained. Louise moved up beside her on the pillows. The smell of Annie's cunt strong around them.

Annie turned the bedside lamp off and held Louise in her arms.

'Do you want to watch the evening news?'

'There is no evening. There is no news.'

They lay whispering sporadically, small things they'd wanted to tell each other. Late night filled the room. Annie pulled the sheet up to cover them and they slept.

Louise woke on her stomach. She felt Annie balancing herself lightly above her back brushing her cunt hairs across her arse. She matched the rhythm. When Annie felt the movement she pressed downward against Louise. The hot lips of Annie's cunt burned against the mound of Louise's arse. Louise pushed upward to meet Annie's clit and Annie quickened her movement. It happened so fast Louise wasn't certain Annie had come. She knew when she felt Annie push her legs apart and heard her say, 'Up!' Louise raised her arse high while Annie continued to move against her. Then she felt Annie's fingers enter her from the rear. She opened wider and began the rocking motion that would cause the explosion. She heard Annie speaking, in a low voice above her ear, telling her how much she needed her, how much she needed to fuck her. She rocked back and forth on Annie's magic fingers. Her clit was enflamed; her cunt was throbbing. She felt as if her body was sucking this woman in.

'Now, baby, now, now, baby.' Annie whispered in her ear

making Louise's body shudder with release. They collapsed on the bed trembling. Deepest night enveloped their sleep.

Louise woke just before the alarm went off at 6.30 am. She rushed into her clothes before Annie had opened her eyes fully. Louise leaned over the bed and turned off the clock radio. She kissed Annie on her mouth then her eyes which were still slightly out of focus.

'I love you.'

'I love you,' Annie said as Louise pulled away and moved to the front door. She glanced back over her shoulder into the livingroom where she'd left the white silk scarf she'd bought for Annie from Third Floor Acessories. Wrapped inside were her cotton panties. They always gave each other gifts. She was back in her own apartment within a half hour and on the way to work, Wednesday morning, on time as usual.

Louise pinned the white, buyer's carnation to her lapel then looked over the order book in the stock room. She could hear the rising voices of customers outside on the floor and the Muzak droning with a perky dullness. The phone rang and her heart jumped. She picked up the receiver. 'Sportswear on Four, may I help you?'

'Yes, I'm trying to find out if you have the Jones of New York blazer in a peach colour ...' said a narrow, nasal voice.

'Yes, we do. Tell me what size and I'll put it aside for you until the end of the day. Your name, please? Fine, they've just come in. I'll have it for you in the stock room. Just come to Four and ask for the white flower.'

DESIRE'S NIGHT OUT

STORME WEBBER

standin posed almost cool/45°
angling away from her half-lidded
eyes/ breath of jasmine honeysuckle
gardenia-scented lips, full and tender
a slight tremble passin through her
as she glimpsed the woman/ self-assurance
emanating with no let up/ feelings, nameless
and heated, flowed through her, tingled her senses
she wanted to know this one more than that
she wanted to possess her and to be possessed in turn.
diva strategy moved into action and she began moving to
decrease that 45° difference. wait. a few more moments
of examination: the woman is handsome, not a masculine but
a strong beauty her features speaking of afrika, and
native american ancient wisdoms travelled through time
and now, resting before her appraising eyes, in lower manhattan
island.
so many lifetimes before this very land that lie far beneath the
concrete
they posed upon was stolen from indian ancestors by english fast
talkers
here and now they stood in this bar of shady origin/ catering to
women like
themselves, ironically called the duchess.
all of this history and reality, seen and felt, swirled around them/just

60

outside of their awareness. inside awareness: sounds — women's
      voices
loud and soft, laughter, fingersnap, 'i wonder if i take you home/ will
you thrill me tonight baby because i need you tonight', the pulse
      of new york
was not left at the door — underlying it all an energy, an urgency,
      a recognition
and need. but now back to our diva. she has passed in front of the
      object of
her fascination/ givin much subtle seduction attitude & just enuf
      scent
of woman, fragrance, desire as she moved on through. she
      continued on
downstairs to spend a few minutes at the mirror/ satisfied with
      what she saw
she moved back up towards her fantasy. the strength in her was
      not lessened by
her lipstick, liner, soft skin revealed and accentuated — sensuous
      power
emanated from each movement and the roll and gentle sway of her
      steps
reminiscent of the mother of all/ earth and sea.

ROUGH TENDERNESS

STORME WEBBER

i need a rough tenderness/ yes
no timid half-stepping romance
but a woman with a sense of
purpose/ direction to her love
a willingness to share openness
some sea of love & comfort
with twenty foot waves of ecstasy
(that still won't drown me lifeless)
a rough suck of an ebb tide
wherein we may rest/ beached
& dripping in amazement
at the luck of two shipwreck
survivors/ come across each other
no robinson crusoe or man friday
not even especially no gilligan's island
no/ instead some sumptuous brown woman
(like the ones that took rousseau on out)
glowing like nature's kiss

THE ART OF POISE

BARBARA SMITH

I lie on my back, head propped up by a pillow and a tender palm. Arms bent, abandoned, wanton, poised and posing. I survey my body, naked, a landscape of undulating breasts and belly, an imagined glistening river of sweat meandering between, amongst and beyond, snaking lazily towards a waterfall of silky moisture between two craggy knees. Legs also bent, feet splayed out, relaxed and at the same time tense because *I spy with my little eye the invited intruder between my thighs.*

We had both been lying, head to toe, sprawled out and yawning on your bed. Mood lighting, mood heightening, we had talked of things I have now forgotten. Slowly we negotiated and re-negotiated the middle of the bed, talking, flirting, shifting and sifting through the possibilities. We maintained our positions whilst transforming our positionings. Your face half-lit by the lamp, half in semi-darkness (can I say that?), of course, your face is as wise and novel as the moon half-caught, both waxing and waning with stars in your eyes. I imagine I was your mirrored twin, also twinkling and sparkling, sparking with mounting desire — mountain desire — and the realisation, the remembering, that *with you all things are possible.* Your words, my memory, you echo, I reverberate.

Which of us will move first? The message flashes, is received, acknowledged, silently we reach a decision.

Whoever gets there first.

Your mouth opens slightly and so it begins. I am object, you are actress. I am looked at and looking, you gaze. But I watch you watching me, and we both know that were we standing you would be on your knees, genuflecting, making obeisance, worshipping me even as I let you control me worshipping you.

But we lie, even as we open each other out and tell and smell the truth, we lie and watch and wait.

A finger fingers me, lingers and manipulates. Brushes hair, grazes lips, teasing clit. Look with your finger-tips. Look, but don't *really* touch, even though the touching of me predates the looking. That comes later. I will come later, you know I will come and how I will come, and test and tease yourself as much as me.

Who is the victim here?

I watch your face watching my cunt. You lick your lips — appetite? Or are you reflecting the movement, the moving of me? Is your face my cunt?

(Later, we will discuss the politics of looking.)

Am I really passive, objectified, unconsenting, deconstructed, feminine and *known*? Are you really active, male and annihilating? But something in me wants the tender touch that will destroy, the betrayer's kiss, the kiss-*off*. I want you to undo me, re-create me, open me up and out like the cliché rose.

Two eyes — one dark, one lit — transfix me; two hands grip strongly my tautly muscled tensing thighs, and manoeuvre me apart. Penetrated and impaled, I comply. Who is moving who, now tell me? Who is moved by whom?

I feel cold breath upon my cunt, making the wetness wetter.

A finger probes me, dips in and takes a surreptitious

mouthful, like a naughty child with frosted icing. Lick, suck, smack, smile — lips and tongue orchestrate the slippery dance.

I watch the delight and pleasure in your face as you open me out and recognize yourself. Pinkly warm glow floods your face, roseate and glistening as the heavy dew on my dawning flower, becoming a flow-er, dribbling from the corners of my mouth, my lips swell and rise to meet yours.

We kiss, face melting into cunt, as candlewax melted into ice along and down my back on some other occasion. Trickled down between my breasts, fiery rain dripping on my breasts, and made puddles of icy fire around my nipples. And, oh! how they stood to attention then!

(But that was another occasion, and later we will discuss the politics of 'burning'.)

Slowly I realize that I am objectifying your face. I ask myself: who is fucking whom? Who is object of the gaze? Who is leader in the dance? Must I move to move you? My hips shudder with questions as the answers fill my cunt, reach up inside to my throat and lie there, strangled and growling. Who cares for answers when the questing is so much more satisfying?

The explosion gathers, rips me out and open, atomizes me, diffuse, dispersed and desiring, I am dissipated into the atmosphere.

(Later, both covered in my fall-out, under a mushroom-cloud of nucleated desire and smoke, we will discuss the politics of dancing and the art of poise.)

NOTHING

CHERYL CLARKE

Nothing I wouldn't do for the woman I sleep with
when nobody satisfy me the way she do.

kiss her in public places
win the lottery
take her in the ass in a train lavatory
sleep three in a single bed
have a baby
to keep her wanting me.

wear leather underwear
remember my dreams
make plans and schemes
go down on her in front of her
other lover
give my jewelry away
to keep her wanting me.

sell my car
tie her to the bed post and
spank her
lie to my mother
let her watch me fuck my other lover
miss my only sister's wedding
to keep her wanting me.

buy her cocaine
show her the pleasure in danger
bargain
let her dress me in colorful costumes
of low cleavage and slit to the crotch
giving easy access
to keep her wanting me.

Nothing I wouldn't do for the woman I sleep with
when nobody satisfy me the way she do.

LIKE A TRAIN

STORME WEBBER

i remember how she/wd fuck
me like a train/inexorably on & on
like the cannonball run
casey at the throttle/& at bat
(but never striking out)
john henry slamming home that sledge/
whipping that machine/pistons driving driving
she wd have me/like that
like stagecoach mary/ambushing my pussy at the pass
(& no i wasn't just along for the ride)
all wet & sweaty like the horses
our flanks heaving/nostrils flared
inhaling that womanfunk
her juice waz my oats, my sweet hay
my clover & sugarlump/all rolled into one
all rolling into one hilarious hayride of a fuck/
one breakneck gallop/pony express don't stop
till we bring it to you/of a fuck
the way bill pickett dogged that runaway bull/
till he dropped/& nat love rode that bronc/
the way we rode each other till one of us gave in or out
& gave a war whoop
& feathers flying/
& engine pumping/& us pumping
& she fuckin me/
like the last steam locomotive
hellbent for pleasure.

GREAT EXPECTATIONS

CHERYL CLARKE

questing a lesbian adventure one splendid night
of furtive, fixed stars and fully intending to have you suck my breasts and fuck me
til dawn called raunchy elizabeth to the window
of your brooklyn apartment saxophone and dolphin-
song muting the rudeness of engines

dreaming the encounter intense as engines
first me then you oh what a night
of rapture and risk and dolphin
acrobatics after years of intend-
ing to find my lesbian sources in the window ·
of longing wide open in me

fearing failing and wanting to do it again faked me
out — anxious wanting revved like 500 engines
inside your brooklyn apartment window
my body a pillar yours a furnace that curious night
of lesbian lore and fully intend-
ing to play an easy rider to your dolphin-
song. instead of asking you to dive on me dolphin-
like, butch stories hushed the lesbian lust in me
across that expanse of sofa and fully intending to make you make me like diesel engines
and taking you back over and over into the night
across your expanse of ass in front of the window.

trading passionate conquest tales and at your window
cobalt night grew pink in the stink, the dolphin
wearying wary of heroics asking for clarity all night
instead of covering face with cunt and entering me
low then spectacularily like rocket engines
you panicked the funky passion i fully intend-

ed. yeah, yeah, a funky passion i fully intended all over the floors walls to the cobalt window
of your brooklyn bedroom till the whine of cold engines
muted the saxophone and called the dolphin
back to sea and your lesbian wetness drying sticky on me
night of furtive, fixed stars oh venus in taurus night.

fully intending to have my way but having no dolphin-
like clarity and the window sticking in me —
a sounding fire engine gridlocked on a windy night.

LETTERS LONG DISTANCE TO A LOVER

ESTHER Y. KAHN

Uno

MALKA SHELI, delicious lover,
With you nothing is ever enough, I want you even when you're not
around ... desire/your fingers ... push me over the edge.

I am sliding downhill, all the way. I want to be fucked,
desperate ... your coat flies out the door before I am awake. Without
your body, heavy on top of me, I am weightless.

You pour out LOVE, so I stand back to mistrust, then I fall
into you. Late at night, on the last train, spelling desire on our
palms, people are watching: we play hermanas latinas, we pass for
whatever is necessary, we pass for so much, in front of those eyes
we speak no english. So we can say 'where we come from women
hold hands and love each other.'

We run in the street, we run behind our front doors, we
eat olives, fuck each other senseless, drowning in wetness, tongues
drawing fruit and juice inside our jewish mouths, a thousand tastes
and memories.

I will seduce you, touch your sex on aeroplanes, shock
families, bite your breast gently ... all soul and open to your
touch ... fuck me with wide open eyes and speak to me.

Today I wear a suit and white shirt, dresses and stockings

embellish the floor, today I wear cologne. I will make you come because you are exciting when you come, deep and electrical.

We raid fruit bowls for things to fuck with ... fresas crushed between our breasts, sweat and juice on our bellies ... you are the most delicious fuck. Lick me, put your tongue in my mouth.

A city hotel, cars screaming past, fragrant/hot, all night, washed in sweat, our fingers tangle, sleekly/sweetly inside each other, I will drink your sex like kiddush wine.

I push you into doorways with my hips and fuck you, the taste of your lips is memory, passion ... lachaim.

What you do to me honey! What I could do to you! Let's make love among the bottles, earrings, letters, fruit skins .... our problems are not in bed ... I can't wash you away.

So we have our tsores, we have our fights, my mother spat in my face, scenes and dramas are nothing new, didn't we all learn the language of pricks? Fantasies and memories mix, the past is part of me ... my imagination cannot intimidate me.

In the arms of you the jew I will let myself be loved.

You have brought out the insatiable and the jealous in me, wanting you at any cost, I will not ask why, throwing things in rage, screaming after you in the streets, I will walk out of restaurants and run back to find you.

Desperate as ever, I will follow you to work, crying and pleading, I will lose my pride. You will be cold so I will hurt you, I will be vicious, and unleash the trait of vengeance. You bring out my traits as I bring out yours.

Jewess sounds like a sexy princess, we are a jewess. You got yourself a hungarian-type princess jewess baby! The mask of stereotype to describe one who is passionate. Tomorrow things will change as they always do in an histoire d'amour. Violinists, gypsies, cantors, daktylas, challahs and red peppers, a black and red skirt, and passion — all I have left of a culture in this cold, cold city.

We have the ashkenazi trait of neurosis to tear us apart when we cannot get out of bed. Even if we are not so ashkenazi we have to get out, because you gotta eat, no?

We go back a long way darling, and of this the white gentiles know next to nothing. So let them decay in ignorance, we will give the kiss of life to our culture. We possess ancestral memories, palms and hibiscus. So, zion fell through, we have our passion, we have our struggle, and I can see a hundred generations of jews in between the lashes and lights of your sexy eyes. Our passion is our culture ....

> Sweet kisses of the tongue,
> rimon, ani ohevotach at,
>
> Esther

◆ ◆ ◆

Dos

Mi querida,

Every time I read about nazis, neo or old style, and they are everywhere, believe me, I react. How? I want to fuck, I become an insatiable jewish woman and a parody of myself. Is this the lesbian version of the jewish obsessions of creating jewish babies? When death is staring you in the face, you cling to life.

I was walking around London, thinking what a sexless vacuum of a culture this is, when I meet this woman, a yiddisher woman who tells me a yiddisher joke ...

The rabbi and the wife of the rabbi go visiting on Shabbat. Moishe knocks on the door and while they wait he kisses the mezuzah, not once but several times with great passion!

'All right,' says Esther, the wife of the rabbi, 'if I hang myself on the wall would you kiss me like that?'

'Tell me,' says the yiddisher woman, 'who doesn't want love! Without love you die.'

I've acted out all the jewish sexual models: I have lusted after retroussés and blond hair; I have lusted after older women; women in the street; women on buses. I have fantasized, wanked obsessively, been a voyeur. I have even shocked myself ... and now in this era of silence?

In this time of knowing who we are but having nowhere to go, what now? I want to fuck all the time, my cunt is a revolution, how meshuggah can you get?

I have absorbed jewish neurosis. I have contemplated jewish obsession and found no answers. I have watched jews in dread of Arabs, jews emigrating to the West Bank, jews desperate for upward-mobility escape routes, and I am here, not liking what I see. But liking you enough to burn up with desire. Have I become obsessed, Rabbi, am I normal?

We could become bored and bicker our lives away in the anglo-saxon rain; sick of neurosis, unable to be thrilled, and no longer frum and perverse, rebellious and sensible, adventurous and practical ... no longer devouring each other day after day? Ay, mi anarchista, que vida.

Everytime I see jews acting like goyim I want to run and have sex. How many of us are still alive?

Let's not talk about it, these are silent years. People will remember these as years of building walls around their lives, we work hard. My taxes are paying for my annihilation, paying the wages of racists and fascists, my taxes are paying for the development of a culture which erases my culture.

Hold me in your arms honey, quick let's make love before we die.

Baila, Viva la Charanga, Olvidar la Pena.

I mean I don't even get depressed, I just turn into a walking metabolizer, Woody Allen has got *nothing* on the average jewish woman, queen of the neuro-erotic.

I ask myself, 'Esther are you a woman or a locust; a plague of locusts?'

The anglo-saxon climate plays havoc with emotions, and nobody pushes me around, me of no ethnicity, me the yid, I push WASPS out of the way because I have no visible traits in their eyes, not that they'll admit it until I push them out of the way. And then they look at me with eyes that say 'you are dirty and a yid.' I look at them and say with my eyes, 'It's about time you looked deep into the eyes of survivors of slavery, of holocaust and take your place. Nobody pushes me around.'

Except you baby. No amount of Estée Lauder could cover the locust in me, it's there in the middle of my face, in my eyelids, in the colour of my lips, for you I am all jew.

Jewish lust is the turn on of your delicious nose, the trait in the middle of your face. I want to make love to your nose.

Honey it is after midnight.

I want you.

Why aren't you speeding towards me on a train

Your breasts warm inside your raincoat

I am always wet for you ...

Esther

◆ ◆ ◆

Tres

Bella,

Without you to talk to, I am crazy. I pick up the phone and rant. I want to talk about love, about music, salsa and rai and klezmer, about politics, about lies and hypocrisy, the sleepwalkers in this city. I want to talk with you about the middle east, about jews.

But we are separated by ambitions, by flaming rows. We are separated by distances, and by our lives.

Sister of my soul, my passionate lover, love of my life always, let's free ourselves, let's do everything! And while we sleep our souls will make love.

Who else can I tell my troubles to? I don't mean to scare you. I am too full of words and ideas to fuck you. Wasn't it easy loving goyim? There was never too much of anything, we were always screaming for something missing. I could never settle for less, I know what is more.

Give it to me.

You never short change me with silence. With you I have more than a pound of flesh, and I don't have to wheeldeal to get it. The world we live in grazes our surface only, we are after all, jewgirls. And all the things which other jewgirls may choose to omit, we, sweet ass, we include. We do not forget.

We see jewboys laugh at Black people and we swallow our fear and ask why: Al Jolson, how could you? My mother says, 'Never ridicule Black people. We are despised and they are despised.' The ghosts of pogrom, holocaust, slavery, the eyes of the WASP have not got to us. We are how we should be: sexual, political and alive.

The black hairs on your golden belly turn me on, your big nose thrills me. The line of your eyelid, the beauty of your cheekbone, the length of your fingers, the words of your mouth ... your traits, they get to me, they turn me on.

Can we drop the jewish mother, jewish princess, jewish neurotics and stop acting like maniacs on vodka with each other? Can we give up on semitic vengeance? Can we be Song of Solomon lovers?

Where is the nice jewish girl? There is no such thing. A jew in the goy mould? Never! I can't fit my nose in a sherry glass, I drink from the bottle. I can throw insults like a challah-baker throws dough, with skill.

I remember my mother screaming in the rain; the uncontrollable, the jew.

Will we ever be less than desperate on this bitter colonial island, or do we get more meshuggah with age?

We still have our jewish asses, and we walk from the hip. We are not running scared. We do not forget.

Come back to me and this bitter city, you know I'm addicted to stimulants: you are one of them, the most intoxicating. I want to wake up in the night with your violet tongue between my purple lips. Enough of shreds, ashes, empty nights, regret, come back and we'll fuck so deliciously, so sweetly, with such intensity, we will never wreck each other's lives again.

Excuse me if I am a walking psychodrama, I can't help myself. I want you and nobody else. What if you are falling in love with someone else, right now, in a nightclub, your lips on her neck, your tongue in her mouth ...

I'll lose control again ... and what is love doing for me ... huh, huh, huh?

Just come back, let yourself into my flat, wake me up ... and really fuck me.

Esther

PROLOGUE

Oh baby, Oh honey, Oh lover ...
An old friend, a gay man, asked me if lesbians were into sex.

'Of course,' I said, 'but I do speak for myself.'

'I thought you were mostly into cuddles and knitting,' he said.

'You're just being bitchy! You want us all to be queens!'

'Where are the women who come out as women?' he asked.

'Everywhere,' I said, 'but we haven't got 'round to talking straight about sex yet. There's SM dykes, muesli monogamists, camp queens and clones and we're talking ... right!'

I want adventures, the more we are sexual, the more we are fighting back. I would rather have wild sex than knit or watch TV.

I want sex which carries me away and changes me ... maybe I am obsessed. Despite the lies, trash, greed, cold and crazy I am going somewhere, with you honey.

I will love you in my bed, soul lover. I will bite your neck, tear at your buttons, pull at your zips. I will open my door and haul you in.

We fuck in the hallway. You ram your fingers inside me, I want you with intensity. Push my skirt up around my waist, slide your fingers into my sex. Your excitement turns me on. I pull at your belt and buttons, plunge my hand into the wetness of you, beyond your delicious rough hairs.

We tangle our emotions, we fuck for hours and find ourselves in different rooms. We scream as we come.

I love it when you seduce me.

I am free of confusion. No WASPS in my mind tangling

up my feelings and desires making me 'other'. I am no longer turned on by myths and innocence ....

I wait for your hand, my sweet jewish lover, to pull me sweetly, irresistably into you.

Viva revolucion,

E

♦ ♦ ♦

Glossary

Malka sheli ... my queen (Hebrew)

Hermanas latinas ... latin sisters or chicas (Spanish)

Fresas ... strawberries (Spanish)

Tsores ... problems, sorrows (Yiddish)

Histoire d'amour ... love story (French)

Challah, daktyla ... bread (Hebrew, Greek)

Ashkenazi ... european jew (Hebrew)

Rimon ... pomegranate (Hebrew)

Ani ohevotach at ... I love you (Hebrew)

Mi querida ... my darling (Spanish)

Mezuzah ... amulet on doorposts of jewish homes (Hebrew)

Frum ... strictly kosher (Yiddish)

Mi anarchista ... my anarchist (Spanish)

Goyim ... white non-jewish people (Hebrew/Yiddish)

Baila, viva la charanga, olvidar la pena ... *dance, viva the charanga,* (a latin dance rhythm) forget your troubles (Latin American Spanish)

Bella ... beautiful (Italian)

Song of Solomon ... erotic poems expressing love and passion and desire as a reference to the jewish idea of god.

Meshuggah ... crazy (Yiddish)

IF IT DOESN'T HAPPEN SOON

CAROLINE TRUSTY

As we talk you are animated: you talk a lot; you use your hands a lot. I have a contradiction of feelings as I respond to you. In one way I feel welcomed, Natalie. You smile a lot. Your real smile. That smile could be your way of keeping your distance. Warning me not to come too close. Being friendly to avoid being friendlier. I don't know which of these feelings are mine and which are yours. Your body tells me that you want to touch me. You lean towards me. As your hands move they move towards me, but if I move to you, they withdraw. Not yet. Not yet.

You talk more and I listen, as our relationship has established. You too know when your talking is keeping you safe. Your apparent openness is your protection against letting go of things that really matter. I know that behind those words is something that says little and means much.

You go to the kitchen to make coffee. I follow you. I feel the need to keep up the momentum that I have created. I don't know if you know it's there, but if I can believe it then maybe it will be.

I watch your movements. I feel your strength. I know that you have too much power right now. Your power could control me — if you are aware of that power. I know that I want to kiss you. I want you. I do want you very, very much.

80

I don't kiss you. You move back. You tell me about your work. I know that you are aware of what could have happened. What you are saying is a veneer on your real feelings and you are not prepared to say anything about those real feelings. I know that if I don't do something, nothing will happen and we will both be left wondering. If it doesn't happen soon it never will.

But I am afraid, afraid of rejection, afraid that if we get involved our expectations won't be met. We may feel passion now, but sometimes wanting is better than having, and I'm still not sure of what I want to have. Is it my lack of confidence that makes me doubt the feelings that I know you have because I can feel them? Or are these feelings a response to the compliment, something that can't hold when something actually happens?

When you talk to me you express yourself so clearly. You seem so honest. I can't quite believe in that yet. I haven't learnt to trust you. However honest you are you won't be honest now. You won't sit there stroking the cat, drinking your coffee and say,

'Maria, I really fancy you, let's go to bed.'

You won't, I'm glad you won't, you shouldn't. Because whether the wanting is better than the having or not, I am enjoying the anticipation that is frustrating and exciting me. I am suffering under that gladly, only because I know that it has to happen soon. If we let it go, the right time will be gone and we will never become lovers. Now it is night, and these are the last few hours we have.

You have created a distance around yourself — emotionally, with your lively talk about our friends, your friends, my friends — physically, with a shift in your chair that would make it awkward for me to get closer to you. If you didn't want me, it wouldn't need that, if there was no interest, we could be more personal.

The shift in your mood accompanies your physical shift that has been towards me, away from me, around me. You have made a decision. You make an issue of the changing of the record. You don't *need* to get closer to the fire.

When you come back from the loo you stand behind my chair, your hand just behind my shoulder. I know that this moment will be lost like all others if I tell myself you don't really fancy me, that it's my imagination, that you fancy Ruth much more, that you're just being friendly, that I am not attractive enough, that I'm not lively enough, that you haven't got over your last lover, that you have taken a vow of celibacy, that you are secretly straight.

So I don't tell myself anything.

I take your hand in my hand, take my courage in both hands and gently pull — not too much to my surprise you follow your hand and come close to me, and as I kiss you I wonder what I was so worried about.

When I kiss you I am aware of every part of me, every part of you. I feel so sensitive to every movement and touch. The softness of your lips, your hair. Natalie, you are such a beautiful woman. What I am feeling now is such a deep satisfaction of desires, made all the stronger by the tentative moments before we felt strong and free enough to do this. I am feeling vulnerable to you, more so than ever because I have never gone into a sexual relationship loving so much before. The sexual feelings I have, have been inspired by the warmth and commitment you have given me.

If you are feeling vulnerable too, you do not say it. You have said you love me — as friends do, I thought. I did not see more in it at the time. I do not now. I could never say I love you, when I was saying everything else to fill the gaping hole made by not saying it. Sometimes it becomes too late. I won't leave it too late, Natalie.

My tongue is caressing yours, your full lips engulf mine. Your teeth bite my tongue in playful motion and I look at you. Your green eyes shining, those delicate fingers holding my face to pull me to you. I feel your breath in my hair, teeth on my ear, tongue running down the nape of my neck. I am shivering and big and beautiful and I feel you pushing yourself towards me, you want me as much as I want you.

As I undress you, I feel the soft curve of your breast at the side of your body. Your skin is so smooth and sensitive. I put my mouth on your nipple. I can feel it hardening beneath my tongue and between my teeth. How close I want to hold you, and so tight, feeling your breast under my mouth and under my hand. I will feel every inch of you with my tongue. Your tongue is stroking the corner of my ear, flicking around my earlobe. Your fingers are in my hair, gently tugging. When I kiss your mouth again I feel your lips, teeth, tongue all responding to me.

As all my clothes are taken away I am finally totally exposed to you. I feel that you could take away layers of my skin. Open to your touch, each layer inspires a reaction as all the tension that has built up in me runs away, like sweat running down my stomach, as you rub against me. Your nails gently scratch my back and your thigh creates a warm pressure between my legs.

When you move, that warm pressure is replaced by your hand, fingers stroking downwards, feeling the wetness that is pouring out of me, gradually slipping in. Inside I am warm and wet and want you. My whole body moves around your fingers, my muscles responding to your movements, clenching you. You kiss me all over, linger on my mouth, feeling the same sensation with your tongue as with your fingers.

As your fingers explore me they find the most sensitive place, and stay there and as I feel intense heat, or cold, it doesn't feel real then nothing feels real. I feel so good my muscles create a great tension, soon to be released. Your kisses turn to bites. I am rising, unable to feel anything else, I push myself closer to you, I want to melt into your body as I scream and tremble and feel fire.

I wrap my legs around you and hold you to me as close as I can. I want your skin against my skin, your breasts against mine. Looking into your eyes is like seeing you for the first time, with an expression I have never seen, saved for your lovers.

Oh Natalie, you look soft and happy. I know that you have become half-satisfied from making love to me and that the rest is waiting, as I stroke you all over, with my fingertips, feeling the fine down along your back, the strong muscles in your legs. The hair between is warm and damp. I bend down to you, breathe your warm smell, trace your thigh with my tongue. As I give you my fingers I see your body engulfing them and when I find you with my tongue you allow me to find a rhythm which is slow, intense, then finds a peak. You raise your body to my tongue, and down onto my fingers. I wish I could see your face as you cry out and I feel your body leaping around my fingers.

Soft sighs, Natalie, so much of you is soft, your smile, your sighs, your body. You have given me so much, by your actions: given me desire, and fulfilled. Love, which I can return. As we lie and talk for hours I feel that connection that our bodies have increased.

I have held you in my arms and woken with you beside me, but never like this.

MONOPOLY

DIANE BIONDO

'Casey,' Leah said, 'I think you gotta be philosophical about this.'

'Hey?' Casey dropped her piece of cold toast and looked up.

'Don't think I'm not sympathetic. I am. Believe me when I say I am very sympathetic to this situation.'

'But?' Her coffee was cold too.

'There *is* a but, it's true. You gotta let it go and be finished. Adios already.'

'Why?' she said, just for the hell of it.

'Are you asking me why? Because these things happen!'

'Relationships end.' Casey took her cigarettes from her bathrobe pocket and lit one up. Leah took one from her.

'Yes they do, they end. No thanks,' she refused a light, 'I only wanna hold it. If they are not meant to be, they end.'

'Is that what you'd say if Barbara walked out on you?'

'Yeah, I think I would.'

'Yeah, I think you wouldn't.' Casey pulled her rope tighter around herself and thought, you'd crumble like a cookie if Barbara left you. That we-are-independent-let's-not-live-together number doesn't fool me. You live for these weekends, are oblivious to others when you're together, and have sex every chance you get. She remembered last Sunday morning, coming into the kitchen and there they were, in one chair, Barbara on Leah's lap, their bathrobes open with nothing on underneath, kissing each other like there was no one else in the room wanting breakfast.

Casey inhaled deeply, stubbed the cigarette out, sighed and rose to clear the table.

'Oh leave the damn dishes, Casey!'

Suddenly Leah had pushed back her chair and, when Casey looked, was glaring at her, which made Casey's mouth open a little in surprise. They stared at each other and Casey, feeling stared down and weakened by it, had to sit again. Leah's cheeks, the colour of a summer tan all year round, had flushed a dark pink, so Casey could tell she was embarrassed by her outburst, but not embarrassed enough to explain or modify it. Instead she said,

'You can't just not eat, you can't just stay in the apartment and drink by yourself. It's tedious.'

With two of her fingers, Casey pushed some crumbs away from the edge of the table.

'I'll try and find a place as soon ...'

Leah was up now and had the tap on full blast. She squeezed the liquid into the sink with one hand, dumped the dishes in with the other. The hot lemon bubbles rose dangerously close to overflowing.

'Gimme a break with the self-pity stuff.'

'It's not self-pity.' Casey sat up straighter.

Leah pushed the sponge around the table, sending all the crumbs to the floor.

'Why don't you say if I'm taking up your space?'

Leah turned off the water, snapped up the dish towel and turned to face Casey who was standing now, but keeping the chair between them.

'Come to the bar with us tonight.'

'I can't.'

'Come and pick someone up!'

'Are you kidding me?'

'Why not?'

'I'm not like that.'

'Like what? Me and Barbara met there!'

'Yeah. Well. One happy couple in sixty thousand meets in a lesbian bar. Proven fact.'

'You gotta try something. Start small. Do something fun.'

Something fun. That'll be the day! Things that were fun seven weeks ago were not fun now. And even if they were, she couldn't do them because she'd already done them all with Ruth. Gabriella's on Seventh for cappuccino, the curry place on Cedar Street, Bernstein's, where Casey derived sensual pleasure from watching the mustard from a reuben sandwich drip down Ruth's chin. Did they ever do anything but eat she wondered, and then remembered the park and the duck pond and how they never had any stale bread at home so they had to feed the ducks with fresh bakery bread bought that morning.

Remembering the park and especially the ducks with their little chicks following single file behind, she had to sit again. If she didn't keep back the tears, Leah would leave the room, so she squeezed her eyes shut and tried to think of something positive to say. But the tears were already there, running down her cheeks, onto her lips, and before they had a chance to roll off her chin, Leah was gone. In a rush of anger, she fantasized tearing the tiles off the wall, breaking a window, kicking the garbage over. Instead she slammed her fist down on the table, but it made such a bang that she startled herself and jumped, coming immediately to her senses.

The routine of Leah's weekends were familiar to her now. In fact, if things weren't what they were, living with Leah might have given her a sense of pleasure and security. She liked the way Leah seemed tied to her habits (Ruth was so spontaneous and unreliable), so that Friday night meant pizza in front of the television, Saturday was laundry day, and of course, Saturday night and all day Sunday belonged to Barbara.

Casey glimpsed the denim jacket and the brim of the black felt hat as Barbara slid past her door, her overnight bag slung over her shoulder. If only we hadn't lived together, she thought of Ruth and repeated the litany of 'if only's'. If only we'd tried harder to keep it fresh by decreasing the frequency of time spent together, prioritizing quality not quantity. If only, like Leah and Barbara, we'd at least pretended to be independent!

Already Leah and Barbara were laughing and behaving like last weekend was two years ago, undressing each other as they moved down the hall. If only the shower wasn't running and the bathroom wasn't so close to Casey's room. If only they wouldn't. Just for once.

Casey sat on the edge of the bed, leaned forward on her knees. Over the sound of the water hitting the bath and the hiss of the heat and steam she could hear them. The deep long groans began quietly, then grew louder, punctuated by purring whispers and sudden sharp intakes of breath. It was time to go for a walk. But instead of heading for the door, she went to the wall and stood very still, touching the barrier lightly with her hand.

A soft sucking noise penetrated the wall. Leah let out an uninhibited moan. Although her eyes focused on a patch of peeling paint, Casey could see what was happening. Barbara had her mouth on Leah's neck. When Leah squirmed, Barbara moved along the bone of Leah's naked shoulder, kissing and sucking her skin until she found Leah's breast and took it in her mouth. Across the rest of Leah's body, Barbara's hands moved, stroking her back, her legs, her arse.

'Let's get in the shower,' she breathed.

'We'll drown!' Leah answered.

They stepped into the bath.

'It's hot!'

'I'll give you hot.'

Suddenly they were shouting to hear each other over the water. Casey realized where she was standing and hurried back to the bed.

'Oh baby, it's just right,' Barbara's voice was in slow motion.

Leah replied, 'Let's do this forever ....'

God forbid, Casey thought, that she should sit alone on this spot forever, while on the other side of the wall, two women stood naked and embracing in the wet heat, their breasts touching, their fingers inside each other, soap and hot water running down their backs. I got to get out of here. But she laid down instead.

'Oh I want it now ...'

'Not yet ...'

She drew her knees up to her chin. Damn them.

'A little faster, yes! It's good ...'

She grabbed the pillow, to put over her head, but held it to her cheek.

'Please, Leah!' Barbara's breathing was a locomotion gaining speed.

'Now, honey ...'

'Move in, Leah ...'

'I can't ...'

'Oh SHIT!'

'Don't stop!'

'I have to!'

'Let me get the ...'

Leah's voice broke off as the water caught her breath. There was a beat of silence in which Casey sat up and took in her own breath. Then, like a bursting pipe coughing and spitting, their laughter escaped and flooded the room.

'I tried to save it!' Leah choked.

'Oh really!'

'Turn that water off and come here ...'

'Talk about passion down the drain!'

It was quiet. Casey blinked. Forcing herself to move, she saw that she'd had the pillow in her mouth and a whole patch of it was wet with saliva. She tossed it aside in disgust, noted that her palms were wet. What's the matter with me? She rubbed her hands together. She wanted to get up, but felt a little shaky. I am acting very stupid, she told herself, and then with horror realized her underwear was wet, that she was aroused and her cunt was responding. She was furious. She cursed them for flaunting themselves and for their lack of consideration and shame, but was just as confused with this reaction as she was with her response to their love-making. She dragged herself off the bed and moved aimlessly around the room until she caught sight of herself in the mirror. With relief she recognized the look. It was sexual, a wild and wanting look, one that told her the truth about the anger. They could have at least finished what they started.

She hoped everyone wouldn't be decked out in the latest cosmopolitan fashions. Not having planned to go out, none of her shirts were clean. She'd have to keep her sweater on. She hoped it wouldn't be too hot. If she had to leave the sweater on to hide the dirty shirt, she'd sweat and her armpits would stink. She hoped it wouldn't be too crowded, because if her armpits stank, there wouldn't be any room to stand apart. Not that she intended to stand by herself all night. She could have stayed at home and done that.

She paid the cover charge and went through to the bar. No doubt she'd end up hanging with Leah and Barbara all night, although she promised herself she would only paddle their way if all other boats were sinking. There they were at the far end of the very crowded dance floor, grinding slowly to a fast tune, it figures. So much for their life-saving skills.

Start small. Do something fun. She rehearsed the reason for being there. She bought herself a drink. She drank it quickly and got another one. It's not so bad here, she decided, because whether I take my sweater off or leave it on, it's pretty safe, since it's too dark to see the stain and too smoky to smell my pits. Consoled by these thoughts, she looked up and saw the woman she wanted to sleep with. She was standing alone. Casey waited awhile, smoking her cigarette and glancing away when the woman saw her looking. She wished she was wearing a black leather jacket instead of some hairy sweater her sister knitted. She sucked in her breath and crossed the bar.

'Hi,' Casey said.

'Hi,' she answered.

'Are you alone, or is your girlfriend on line in the bathroom?'

'My girlfriend's in another woman's bed,' she replied.

'Oh, that's good.' The woman raised her eyebrows. 'I mean, it's not good for you, though.

'I guess it's good for her.'

'Who can say.'

'I'm sure I'll hear all about it,' she smiled and sipped her mineral water.

Casey couldn't think of anything to say to that, so she asked, 'What's your name?'

'Lou,' she answered, 'Wanna dance?'

Lou was a good dancer. She listened intensely, hearing the beats and anticipating the song's rhythm. Casey hardly heard the music. She was too busy watching Lou who, although taller and heavier than herself, moved her feet, arms and hips in graceful synchronicity. There's something delicate about her, Casey analysed. She has nice curly hair, maybe it's that. It's probably very soft. She suddenly felt self-conscious about her own hair which was short and spikey, and her dancing which seemed to have nothing to do with the music. Luckily, a slow song came on next.

'I'm a better slow-dancer,' she confessed.

'Aren't we all?' Lou wrapped her arms lightly around Casey's back. Slowly, they circled the small space where they stood. Feeling a quick rush of courage, Casey pressed her fingers into Lou's back. Lou understood and moved closer. As they turned in their tiny spot, feeling Lou's breath on her neck, Casey rubbed herself over Lou's thigh. Lou did the same, pushing into Casey's hip, her hands clasped around the small of Casey's back. And so like that they moved, pushing and rubbing into each other from their hips down, until the music changed and they awkwardly moved apart.

'She's one of their better DJs, don't you think?' Casey asked, immediately regretting it, thinking she's probably the only one.

'I think the one on Friday is better,' Lou said. 'Do you want a drink?'

Just then Casey caught sight of Leah, standing at the bar, smiling and waving in her direction.

'Thanks,' Casey handed Lou her beer glass, 'the same.'

Just as Lou turned towards the bar, Leah threw Casey two thumbs-up signs. Casey quickly turned away, hoping Lou hadn't seen that.

Casey took in the details of Lou's apartment. There wasn't a crumb on the carpet. There wasn't a crease in the cover on the couch. She could see her reflection in the turntable cover, and all the books were in alphabetical order, divided into fiction and non-fiction.

'Does your place always look like this or is this just in case of company?' she asked when Lou came out with the coffee.

'It always looks like this,' she answered.

'That's amazing. How do you motivate yourself?'

'It's easy. I hate dirt.'

As if to confirm this, Casey's eye came upon the THANK YOU FOR NOT SMOKING sign.

'Oh shit,' she said before she could stop herself.

Lou followed her gaze to the notice. 'Do you have to?'

'Yeah, I think so. I'll smoke it fast.' She took out her cigarettes and lit one up. Lou sipped her coffee and looked away.

'Uh, do you think I could have an ashtray?'

Lou went out to the kitchen and came back with the lid to a pickle jar. She handed it to Casey, opened a window and sat down. Casey tried to smoke quickly, but the hurried puffing seemed to make more smoke.

'You and your lover been non-monogamous for long?' Lou asked, coughing a little.

'No. Never. Didn't I say we split up?'

'Not in so many words.'

'Well, it was only seven weeks ago, so.'

'But who's counting, right?' Lou was smiling. 'Was that her at the bar tonight? The woman you were avoiding?'

'Oh, her! That was my room-mate, Leah.'

'You avoid your room-mate?'

'It's a long story. How long have you and your lover been non-monogamous?'

'About two weeks. Nell met this woman in our sky-diving group and I guess it's a big deal for her.'

'You jump out of planes?'

'We use parachutes.'

'Good.'

'You should try it, it's exhilarating.'

'I have trouble with ladders.'

'You don't need a ladder to board.'

'I meant heights.'

'Oh! Heights. Yeah. But this isn't like falling off a ladder. It's like floating. Do you wanna see a picture I took from the sky?'

They moved to the wall where the photograph hung.

'Doesn't everything look small!' Casey was impressed. 'The buildings look like monopoly houses. I feel dizzy just looking at it.'

'That's weird,' Lou stepped back, 'Nell said that. One day we were getting ready to jump and we were looking down and she said, "Louey, that's our Monopoly board down there. Don't believe it's all any bigger than you're seeing it now, 'cause it isn't. It's a small game that goes on for hours.'"

Casey nodded. 'She's a philosopher, right?'

Lou outlined the frame of the picture with her finger.

'I love this picture,' she said.

Casey took Lou's hand and put it to her mouth. She kissed first her fingers, then her palm. Lou stretched out her arm and pulled up her shirt sleeve. Casey kissed her wrist and up her arm which smelled of rose talcum powder. When the shirt prevented her from kissing any further, she kissed her lips. Her first thought was how small Lou's mouth was. She had thin lips and little teeth, which Casey hadn't noticed before because she had been so taken with her soft hair and natural movements. She opened her mouth a little more, encouraging Lou to do the same, but Lou's mouth seemed to be open as wide as it would go. She moved her tongue to find Lou's, but somehow it evaded her.

'Should we go into the bedroom?'

Casey followed, sobered by a rising disappointment and worried by the time she used the bathroom and got to bed, she'd want to go home. Lou was already undressed and under the covers. She could hardly say, thanks for the kiss Monopoly-Mouth, and go! Why did she have to take her clothes off all at once, anyway? The first time Casey and Ruth made love, they kissed for hours, growing more and more excited by the mystery of the covered curves and shapes. They remained dressed until they were sweating everywhere and the clothes felt burning and unbearable and had to be tugged at in a frenzy to get them off and feel the sticky warm skin underneath. But you can't plan these things, she scolded herself and quickly undressed and got into bed.

Immediately, Lou lifted herself and covered Casey with her body. Casey gasped at the sensation of Lou's skin on her's, it was fire-hot. Every part of her was in contact with this soft heat, sending chills up her back. She felt herself go into a moment of shock and lie frozen, like the second in a sneeze when your heart stops.

Maybe there's something to be said for this starting naked technique, she thought. She looks better without that shirt she was wearing, we probably would have lost it if we tried to do it with our clothes on. She's pretty smart I guess, with her let's-get-down-to-it attitude.

Oh my god, she felt Lou's lips on her face, I hope I'm not gonna think through the whole thing. As if to prevent her from doing so, Lou began to move her breasts over Casey's breasts, gently pushing and rubbing. Casey's nipples grew hard and tingled with the desire to be kissed. Sensing it, Lou teased her, tickling the hardened nipples with her tongue, her breasts, moving in and then away from her. Casey moaned and chased her, arching her back to catch Lou's movements, relaxing when Lou came back to lie fully on top of her. When they were moving together, Casey, at last without conscious thought, aware only of her own deep sounds, identified the parts of Lou which were touching her cunt, the rough, spongy pubic hair, the soft skin on the inside of her thigh, the sensation of the pubic bone when Lou pushed down on her. Most of all her senses were alert to the wetness they shared between them. Lou's saliva was running from her own mouth and down her chin. There were tiny beads of sweat between her breasts and Lou's also, and between her legs, where Lou had placed herself, opening her cunt so Casey could find her clitoris with her own, there was a trickle of wetness which flowed between them and belonged to both of them. It stuck to their hair, to the inside of their legs and to the sheet underneath them.

Casey shut her eyes and let the images of river, lake and stream float over her. Sensing her abandonment, Lou cupped her hands under Casey's arse, fingered her buttocks and pushed them up, until the pressure of their cunts together was too much and

Casey climaxed, grabbing for Lou's arse and holding it tightly in her hands.

Lou went for a glass of water.

'I'm real thirsty,' she said. 'Oh, I didn't get you one. Want some of this?' Casey shook her head. Lou slid back down under the sheets.

'Did you come?' Casey exhaled and wiped her face. She cleared her throat, but couldn't form any words. 'Forget it, you don't have to say.'

'I did,' she managed.

'Good. You'll probably want a cigarette now, right? You definitely cannot smoke in the bedroom, okay? Nell just had to have her post-orgasmic smoke or it wasn't worth fucking.'

'Lou,' Casey whispered, 'I'm not ready to talk yet.'

'Okay.'

'No, I mean, why, let's not stop.'

She moved under and drew circles on her cheeks with Lou's nipples. She kissed each breast gently and slowly, touched her stomach which was round and smooth. Recalling the feeling between her legs when they danced, she slid down the length of the bed. She ran her hands up the inside of Lou's thighs, she played with Lou's pubic hair, circled her cunt, looking for the opening, waiting for the wet welcome to happen between her fingers. She breathed in the scent of Lou's sex and was excited again.

The months she'd gone without sex, she hadn't been aware of missing it. Now she felt as if her celibacy had lasted years, her desire and her need to satisfy was so strong. She put her face between Lou's legs and kissed her, opened her mouth on her and wanted more. She slung her cunt over Lou's leg and moved on it, worried she moved too fast, but unable to slow herself. When the bed was a boat on a wavey sea and nearing the edge of the world which was flat, her orgasm was seconds away. But how to wait for Lou? The thought of Lou stung her and at once she stopped. Lou lay perfectly motionless and silent under the touch.

'Lou.' she whispered.

'Yes.'

'Do you want me to?'

Lou paused and answered, 'I'm sorry.'

Casey fell on her back like she'd been punched. The blood rushed chaotically through her limbs then to her head which started to pound. Her skin hurt. Feeling naked for the first time, she rolled on her side, tightly pressing her legs together to stop the expectant throbbing there.

They were silent for some time. When Casey was sure the sensitive electric field around her body had begun to thicken, she moved up to the top of the bed. They lay on their backs and stared into the dark ceiling. Finally, Casey asked,

'What are you thinking, Lou?'

'I was thinking about sky-diving.' she answered.

'It's very commendable of you, telling me the truth like that.'

'You're probably gonna think this is weird, but I enjoy sky-diving more than, more than sex. It's just so, I don't know, uncomplicated. Do you think that's crazy?'

'Yes.'

'Sex is like this thing you do to get out of yourself, it's abandoning yourself, right?'

'For some of us it is,' Casey said sharply.

Lou ignored this and went on, 'But it's not very real. Parachuting is the opposite. It's pleasure that comes only if you're really with it. You gotta concentrate and be aware of yourself and the world below. Sense of timing is crucial.'

'Sense of timing is crucial in sex, too. Holding off that little bit longer, drawing out her pleasure to its maximum, holding off until, whoosh! away she goes, just like I did to you. I'm not usually a sarcastic person,' she added.

'Don't be mad,' Lou said.

'Are you going parachuting with Nell today?'

'Yes, why?'

Casey threw off the cover with a sweep of her arm. 'I better go home.' Lou touched her arm.

'Go home?'

'I don't feel so good.' She got out of bed and put her T-shirt on.

'Is it 'cause I said I was seeing Nell?' Casey stood by the bed holding her socks. 'Are you jealous? No, you couldn't be!'

'Why not?' Her voice was louder than she expected.

'Because we only just met, I guess.'

'So? Don't you have feelings?'

'Yes!'

'Why did you invite me back here, anyway? You didn't really like me, did you?' She glanced around for her underpants. 'You just wanted to even the score with Nell. You said so yourself, you'll hear all about her night and she'll hear all about me, too! You can't wait to see her and tell her you got fucked last night!' She was crying now and couldn't stop herself.

'Oh, don't cry,' Lou tried to touch her, but Casey shrugged her off.

'What's so great about this paratrooper, anyway, you can't lose yourself in me for one night? And don't try and tell me you have multiple orgasms when someone pushes you out of a plane! You just think you're the only girl in the world that's been ditched, that's what. You're not, you know. Others are ditched, too, but some of us try and have fun and some of us just lay there thinking about sky-diving.'

Casey tucked on both her socks, but still hadn't found her underwear.

'Look, I'm not used to this kind of thing,' Lou examined a dangling thread on the blanket, 'I never picked anybody up before.'

'Oh yeah?' Casey's mouth was hanging open. 'And what do you think, I do this all the time, this is my hobby?'

'But you were so confident ...'

'Hah!' Casey got on her knees and pulled her underpants out from under the bed. She shook them off even though there was no dust, and put them on. 'Anyway, you did all the smooth talking.'

'I watch a lotta movies. But you seemed to know the real thing, you really got into it ...'

Casey saw herself on top of Lou, sucking her cunt, rubbing herself along her leg, out of control, all the while Lou was unmoved. Fresh tears of embarrassment rose in her throat and choked her. 'Why did you have to say that!'

'I meant it as a compliment, you're very sens-'

'Why didn't you stop me? I could have gone on and done it to you and you wouldn't have stopped me.'

'Why should I stop you?'

'Because you didn't feel anything. How do you think that makes me feel?'

'You seemed okay.'

'For gods sake, didn't you care nothing was happening to you?'

'No.'

'Well, you made a fool of me. I feel like shit.'

Casey struggled with her jeans. She got one leg in but it was the wrong one.

'I wish you wouldn't go home,' Lou said. Casey reached for her shoes, sniffling. 'It's real late. I wish you'd stay. We could talk.'

'You wanna tell me why you're a compulsive cleaner?'

'You can't go out like that, you're all upset, you'll get mugged.'

'There's nothing left to take.'

Lou rolled her eyes but didn't comment. Instead, she removed a bottle of brandy and two glasses from the dresser beside the bed.

'You'll like this,' she said, 'You should have some. Especially if you're thinking of going home, it'll warm you up.' She poured two glasses and set one aside for Casey. When Casey didn't move, she said, 'Go get your cigarettes from the living room and come back. I'll let you smoke in here, if you want.'

Casey checked Lou's face to see if she meant it. When she knew she did, she pictured the crumbless living room carpet, the perfectly pressed couch cover, the dustless floor under the bed, the red and white THANK YOU FOR NOT SMOKING sign. She imagined the smoke blowing on the pink bedroom curtains, polluting the purely breathable air. For days afterwards, Lou would have to sleep in a room stinking of stale cigarette smoke. She sat on the edge of a chair and dug in her pocket for a used tissue. She blew her nose. Was this Lou's attempt at reconciliation, maybe even friendship? She felt it was some sacrifice Lou wanted to make for her, small as it was. She saw the brandy out of the corner of her eye. It would be sweet and warm. She wanted it with her cigarette under the bedcovers. Lou was waiting.

A strong sense of having won something came over her. Inside, her hopes said she'd regained her dignity and her self-confidence. But the reality of the outside world, small as it may have seemed to some from the sky, told her the victory was only the result of a rule being broken on her behalf.

'Okay,' she said, 'I'll go get them.'

Small, but a victory nonetheless.

'Don't forget the pickle lid!' Lou called.

CRAZY ABOUT MARY KELLY

CHERRY SMYTH

The first time Janine made love with Caragh she was shocked. As she unbuttoned her shirt and eased it off her shoulder to lick and kiss the skin, she saw freckles everywhere. Janine felt an uncanny rush of tenderness for this woman she had just met. She recognized something in the way Caragh's hands held her body.

That night they had left the club together and got nervously drunk on Jameson's at Janine's. Caragh drank her whisky hot, soaked with cloves and lemon; Janine liked her's straight with ice. Their ears still buzzing with loud funk, both women continued to flirt with the thrill of anonymity. The taste of whisky and the sense of familiarity gave Caragh strange courage and she pulled Janine from her chair and seated her firmly on her lap.

'You're completely stocious, so you are!' Janine had laughed.

'Where did you learn that expression?' Caragh had asked suddenly, reminded of somewhere else. Reminded of her father, thin and broken, standing by the back door, shouting at her:

'Raised for the boat, all of yous. Sure they took all the good land, left us nothing but bog of stoney oul ditches.'

She had left Donegal that winter and come to London for work.

Caragh was unnerved that Janine's words had summoned such vivid images of the past. She was unexpectedly moved and very turned on. She clutched Janine's open-necked shirt and made a fist, pulling her towards her mouth — a hard full kiss which tried to find the words Caragh could not release. They broke apart. Surprised, Janine said,

'My Aunt Edie would say that. She came over years ago and never lost her Ballymena accent.'

'What d'ya expect from an' ol' Prod. They never let go, do they?'

They did not contact each other for weeks after that night. Neither of them willing to acknowledge it had happened, that it had made them feel so unexpectedly raw.

Janine felt angry a few days later. She could no longer concentrate on writing her article.

That bitch won't ring, she decided. It was all some big challenge to fuck me, fuck some idea of Englishness she can't stand. So arrogant and defensive. To laugh at how I pronounced 'cup of tea'. She emanates rage and I don't even know where it comes from, but somehow I'm implicated. She looked so relaxed when she was dancing, as if she saw nothing around her, just wrapped in her own pleasure. Her hips. The way she moved her hips as she lay taut and strong above me, her cunt drawing me in, her eyes growing larger, the pupils darker. I wanted to bite her, slap her for looking like that.

Janine remembered how Caragh had raised up and sat on her fist, touching her own breasts with those long, thin fingers, rolling them roughly in her hands, pushing them together and looking so distant and proud. So proud she could not get that face out of her head. Then Caragh had drunk and kissed her and water had poured from her mouth all over Janine's stretched and made-beautiful body. Janine rolled on her and wanted to press herself into her totally, everywhere. She moved on top of her and sucked at the fold of her armpit and bit her nipple and circled her hip over Janine's cunt, and she wanted her inside. Her flesh was wet with sweat and more desire as Caragh fucked her deep and long, pushing her off the edge of the bed and onto the floor, still fucking, lifting her hips up, opening her wider — she was hers, hers to do whatever she wanted. Caragh looked invincible above her, almost untouchable in her power. It made Janine weak, beyond speech. She lay hot and sleepy and emptied. Caragh drew her gently back onto the bed, wrapped her up and held her close.

I can't get that face out of my head. Yet she was so cold in the morning. So closed. She seemed guilty. I'm not going to ring. That wasn't the deal.

Caragh soaped her son in the bath. She rested her hand beneath his neck and swam his small body up and down in the water. Finn giggled. His dark skin gleamed. She stood him up and lifted him out. As she dried him, she remembered how Janine had washed her in the shower, the way she had looked at her skin and kissed her shoulders. How she had taken her hand and placed it in her own swelling and soaking cunt.

'Touch her,' Janine had whispered, 'see how ready she is.'

Then she had turned her round to face the wall and pressed her body up against Caragh's. 'I resisted,' thought Caragh, remembering the force with which she'd pushed against Janine. Her arms were spread apart, her hands flat and defiant against the tiled wall. She felt too exposed, unable to lose herself.

She said she hadn't seen me before; but I'd seen her. I used to watch her at those talks she gave on lesbian politics. Cocky bitch. Fucking hell, I bet she thought she'd slum it with me. 'Janine Robertson, academic, with a special interest in the Irish question.' I didn't tell her about Finn. It was like playing a part — unattached, unconcerned. I had control. I was anonymous.

She was moving her hands over my arse. I wanted to make her beg to touch me, I made her say please; say my name; say please again. Then I wanted her. I wanted her to lick me. She knelt down and licked the crack between my cheeks, her hands pushing the top of my buttocks, holding me firm and sure, making me safe. I didn't want to be safe. She was so sure of herself. I wasn't going to trust her. Yet I was wet. How was I so wet?

Then I wanted her like a rage — an anger in my arms, my head, my chest, my legs — it didn't even seem to focus in my cunt where her hand was — it was driving me, pulsing through me and I wanted all of her body in me, over me, under me. I've never felt that kind of desire before. It felt crazy and insatiable. I wanted to smash my head against hers, bash my arms against the wall, make her knead the flesh of my thighs to let out the rage of want. I wanted to fight her, to wrestle, be broken. I had never let anyone take me beyond control like that; I needed her past coming.

And I fucked her hard and she wanted it that way. She couldn't be filled enough. Her eyes grew wide and greedy. I drove my hand in her and she looked magnificent. She came like a storm. Huge cries and her body shaking. There are small bruises darkening on my arms where she clung to me.

I *am* good enough to fuck her, that was the challenge. That was all I wanted. So why does she still bother me? After we fucked and laughed and talked, all I had set out to prove collapsed, irrelevant. I liked her.

◆ ◆ ◆

Caragh rushed into the cafe to shelter from the rain and began to queue at the counter. Her coat and bag dripped. Her hair felt cold and flat around her face. She was not particularly hungry. She ordered soup and a roll and then looked around for a table. She noticed the back of a woman's head, bent, reading one of the gay magazines that lay about the place. The bones at the bottom of her neck stood out above her collar. Caragh felt excited and sick. The seat opposite her was empty. Janine's hand turned the page. Caragh went and stood at the edge of the table.

'Can I join you?' She tried to make her voice even.

Janine's face lifted. Her eyes registered and her expression brightened suddenly, then calmed again. Her mouth twisted in an ironic smile.

'Please do,' she said dryly.

Caragh shivered inside and a little burst of wet exploded in her knickers. She had forgotten how resonant Janine's voice was. Her top lip curled and her mouth stayed slightly open after she had spoken. Caragh could feel her palms moisten and sweat prickle under her arms. She made tight fists under the table and breathed deeply into her stomach. She managed to begin eating although she tasted nothing. She wanted to touch Janine's hand, to hold the side of her face, to press her head hard into her body. She did not hear Janine's words — what she had eaten for lunch, what she liked about the new decor in the cafe — her voice reached into Caragh's cunt, but the meaning of the words did not filter through the desire.

As Janine began to roll a cigarette Caragh saw that her fingers shook.

'She actually seems nervous,' thought Caragh. 'Does she feel this want? Is she aching? Does she see my shame? Shame for hating and wanting to fuck what she stood for; and shame for needing her like I did.'

Janine drew in a long breath of smoke and looked at Caragh's eyes. They were clearer and deeper than she had remembered. The whites were almost blue. She tried to keep cool, to disguise from Caragh her surprise and pleasure at seeing her again.

'It must be four weeks,' she thought. 'It seems like months. I can't bear not referring to it. Why must we be so private after such intimacy? I want to take her by the hand and lead her down to the toilets and fuck her now. She's less angry. She's not fighting me anymore. It feels different.'

'It was too close to the bone,' began Caragh.

'Yes, I know.'

'Not really what I expected, I suppose.'

Janine smiled.

Caragh went on, 'There seemed to be so many emotions brought up between us — from nowhere.'

'I can't let you go,' Janine said firmly.

Their eyes met and held for a moment, both startled by the urgency and determination in Janine's words.

'What are you doing later?' she continued, more light-heartedly.

'Picking up my child, going home, making tea, putting him to bed and then seeing you.'

'Good,' said Janine slowly, her face relaxing. 'We have to talk. I have to tell you about Mary Kelly.'

'Who's she?'

'A girl from Derry in my primary school who'd gaps between her front teeth, bony fingers and lots of freckles.'

'Did you love her?'

'I was crazy about her. Other kids teased her. She used to pull her finger joints until they cracked and then practise making fists. She was always getting ready for a fight. But her preparations would scare everyone away!'

Caragh laughed.

'I've a few stories to tell you too,' she said.

SATURDAZE

LIANN SNOW

Ms Delia Sandsome never could get good sex. Except on Saturdays and even then only between one and three in the afternoon. Delia searched for sex and found it in its many forms, but good sex she could find only with Sardine, a skinny, slippery, sallow-faced, fine-haired, breastless, fifteen-year-old member of the female sex.

On Saturdays Sardine went fishing. Off the docks, her family thought, but Sardine fished in deeper waters. Delia Sandsome, beached pink-breasted on a foamy white bed, her body laced, pinched and puckered with satin (black or mauve), her perfect heart-of-a-face glowing at the cheeks and blowing at the mouth, was catch enough for skinny Sardine, who darted like a silver fish between her cushiony thighs. Oh yes! Well worth waiting a week for.

Zip, zip, zip went Ms Delia's legs, her toes neatly pointed as sharp as scissor blades. Slip, slip went Sardine, sliding in and out of satin flesh and fabric. In, in, in she went, sometimes so far that she nearly lost her way, but always there was a familiar hill, hollow or curve that helped her, oh so very slow, backtracking retreat, withdrawal, exit, escape from the labyrinth. Once she thought she saw a bull's horn lamp lit to light her way, but she never told Delia that. She never told Delia much at all. Sardine's family weren't the only ones who didn't know where Sardine was of a Saturday afternoon.

Sometimes Sardine found a pink pearl in an olive grove and held it in her mouth, rolled it round her tongue and sucked it with pursed lips, or slid it along the slit of her mouth, and then Delia held the back of Sardine's head and rolled her head around on it. Sardine loved the shiny pink pearl.

Other times, Ms Delia Sandsome grew muscles in her arms and thighs. Her body hardened as she lay upon the open body of the girl and the pearl magically grew, they knew not how, and it sprang out of its nest and pierced her. Many times Ms Delia penetrated the young girl's flesh, spreading her nether cheeks with firm, strong hands; also, on some velvet afternoons, the pearl, now pointed, now coloured cherry red, dipped itself into the sweet waters between the young girl's thighs, and at such times both persons glued themselves in silent joy, lip to lovely lip.

This is good sex! Ms Delia Sandsome thought. But it is not enough. I will find more. Though I haven't yet.

And so Ms Delia S sallied forth in search. But not on Saturdays.

CUCUMBER

CHERYL CLARKE

The texture of cucumber
repulses my lover.
But last night we'd forgot
our toy.
I spied a deep green
firm cucumber
in our hostess' fruit dish.
I stole it to our room.
I made the room dark.
The drums outside became more
than themselves and
syncopated.
I rubbed the perfect cuke with
a ginger oil,
knelt near the bed
and lulled my eyes closed.
The toilet flushed.
Her steps.
I smelled her as she entered
knelt upright before me
and faced me squarely.
Anchoring myself against her
I pulled the crotch of her
bathing suit
to the side

and felt her there, bent
and licked her
to make certain of wetness.
She was surprised at first.
I reassured her she could take it
and soon she had no question.
After, I said with satisfaction:
'I finally learned a way to feed
you cucumber.'

MASTURBATION IS FOR WANKERS

BARBARA SMITH

A brief encounter on a cold June day in Amsterdam. It was raining. We had stopped outside a promising-looking shop near the Waterlooplein when Barbara indeed met her Waterloo.

Why does anyone go to Amsterdam? Tulips, diamonds, and as much perverse sex as possible. A Puritan country but little puritanism to be found. I wanted that irony, that perversity. I was here to break a mould. And all these flights from conformity for some reason seem so much easier, if not expected, in a foreign country. Amsterdam was perfect for the culturally ignorant British tourist: everyone speaks English and not an eyebrow raised in the act of translation. You ask, you get. Nice and easy.

I had been inexorably drawn to social anthropology. Almost my destiny you might say — wonderful archaic rites and rituals fascinated me, especially when I realized that studying far-flung cultures brought me psychically closer and closer home. Rites of passage we knowing Westerners call them, when those who are about to change, are expelled from society, allowed to run riot with one last fling out of childhood, and then are incorporated forever as sober citizens. I wanted my few days of sanctioned sexual anarchy. It comes to us all in the end. So there I was on foreign soil, aching to make concrete the shadows of my soul. A woman is not free until she controls her own orgasms.

One glance in the window was enough. I was decided. After years of closetry, I finally made up my mind.

It wasn't love at first sight. No, you couldn't call it love when I knew so little about it (and know so much less now!). And you couldn't speak in terms of need, since I'd lasted this long without it. It was want, pure and simple. Lust, nothing more than that. A long-felt, often concealed yearning to satisfy a hungry fantasy, to make those dreams a reality. I just fancied it, that was all. And that was all it took. A woman is not free until she has a hand in her own orgasms.

We went inside and held hands as we surveyed the items on display. One monumental decision led to a plethora, back to uncertainty again. She looked at me, eyebrow raised quizzically, inviting me to decide there and then, squeezing my hand in an act of sisterly encouragement that was far from innocent. We separated and wandered round, glancing occasionally at each other, last minute doubts raising the hackles on my neck. Would I regret this? It was a big step. We'd talked about it so often, she always so positive, me curious but always holding back and held back.

My head screamed: this can't go on. Will the real Barbara please come out of the closet? I've got to make up my mind now. This might never happen again. I'd kick myself for passing up the opportunity. I needn't tell anyone. If I don't like it I can stop. This is making me sick.

Okay, let's cut the pseudo-metaphysical tantalizing crap. I went into a sex shop and bought a vibrator.

I had wanted to buy one ever since I'd leant against a spin-dryer and almost came on the spot. Various things had stopped me: the phallic appearance, the cost ...

'Mum, can I have an advance on my pocket-money to buy a vibrator? No, I don't want a Cindy Doll ... Aw mum, Judy's got one ... Waddya mean what do I want it for? No, I can't borrow hers ... Okay, can I borrow yours?' (She said she'd hit me for being argumentative.)

Everyone said they made you numb and were a waste of time and money. The real thing was much better ... What real thing? I only know one prick that hums and he lives next door.

Nothing is ever simple. I think it's called Sod's Law. If something *can* go wrong in any situation, it *will* go wrong. I had gone to Amsterdam with my lover to recover from exams, try and start our rock'n'roll relationship over again (it was rocky, then rolled to a halt), and buy my vibrator. What happened? We split up completely, and I was in the weird situation of buying a vibrator accompanied by my ex-lover. That changed the proceedings completely: instead of being something to expand our sexual horizons, I was going to have to do it single-handed. Not only that, but Sod's Law teaches that you can go through Customs with as much excess duty-free as you like and your chances of being searched are minimal. But if you try and do something legal but embarrassing, like bring in a vibrator, you're bound to be searched.

Something like that anyway. We were coming back on a Sunday. The shops would be shut. I like to eat at least once a day. I brought back some food. We went through Immigration, no probs for my EEC passport but she was American and a Jumbo had just landed from Istanbul. The 'other' queue was phenomenal. She said, 'You go ahead, collect our luggage and wait for me in the Baggage Hall.'

So I went through, grabbed one of the few free trolleys, collected our bags from the carousel. Mine was off first, hers was last. I had to repack the trolley to get it all on. Finally she arrived. We went through Customs, nothing to declare, out of the airport and into the tube station. About to unload and I realized I'd left my duty-frees in the Baggage Hall. Pillock!

What actually got me into trouble was the potatoes — I didn't have an import licence or a phytosanitary certificate. Oh, don't ask, it's something to do with Colorado Beetle and cheap Cyprus new potatoes. The Customs man explained that I was suspected of trying to pull at least one of two common scams — importing cheap potatoes to undermine the Jersey monopoly, or greedily getting two lots of cheap booze and fags.

'You'd be surprised what some people get up to,' he confided wearily. 'People go through Customs once with their allowance, dump it on a friend in the tube station, then come back claiming they've lost it hoping to get an extra bite of the cherry. Goes on all the time.'

I made suitable noises of incredulity. Someone had found my bags almost immediately, easily noticeable by the canary yellow. Of course they searched it — might have been a bomb — and inside, incongruously, they found a bottle of expensive whiskey, two bottles of expensive wine, and 1.9 kilos of new potatoes.

'Sorry, miss,' and he really was sorry. 'I'm going to have to impound the potatoes.'

'What about my duty-frees?'

'Well, technically you've already been through Customs with nothing to declare. You can't go through them a second time, which you'd have to if I let you have your duty-frees. Mind you, you reported the loss within fifteen minutes — that counts in your favour. You say your friend is waiting for you in the tube station? Come on then.'

Believe me, I am cutting a long story short here. The guy marches me back to the tube station where my 'friend' is sweating buckets. Have I been arrested? He goes through my bags, everything is okay till we get to a small parcel wrapped in brown paper. I'd spent an hour trying to persuade this guy I was an upright citizen who wouldn't dream of doing anything illegal, unusual or tempting.

'What's this?' he asked.

'A vibrator,' replied I, trying not to sound sheepish.

'Oh,' he says, ' I don't think I need bother you any more,' as he hastily repacks my bag and shoots off back to petty bureaucracy.

It is with all this in mind that I lie on the bed, legs akimbo, flush with anticipation, vibrator in one hand, dildo in the other.

In these days of AIDS panic, it is still a wise move to check out the sexual history of your partner before embarking on any lustful voyage, then, to be doubly safe, throw a Mae West on it. I knew about the dildo — it had been in and out of trouble ever since I brazenly marched into Ann Summers and demanded two, one each, and the assistant had to ring round all the branches to find a pair in the same shop (Charing Cross Road is your best bet) — but I wasn't so sure of the vibrator. Okay, it might have been a virgin, but look what happened to Mary. Furthermore, condom awareness is fine for heterosexuals and gay men, but what about us lesbians? If safe sex equals condomless-raising, where do we put ours? And if the patriarchy really wants to 'protect' everyone (and it really is the biggest prick in the biggest prophylactic in the world — who will sing the reggae version of the Northern songstress' immortal song at an AIDS aid concert?) then that means it has to acknowledge prickless sex as more than a viable alternative. I'm not taking bets.

As I say, bearing all this in mind, I am about to embark on a voyage of self-discovery. I weigh up the possibilities — and put the dildo back in its holster. Turn on and tune in, my substitute spin dryer starts to trek the voluptuous terrain that is my body.

Actually, landscape imagery really pisses me off with its earth-motherish euphemisms. Forget the rolling hills and deep, dark ravines, virgin fields to be ploughed, etc etc. I plunged the fucker into my cunt.

Not bad actually. I put the KY back as unnecessary.

So I'm rolling around with myself, unleashing my favourite fantasies, whispering disgusting obscenities in my ear and really turning myself on. I never knew I was so good. Until you learn to love yourself, they say, you can't love anyone else. Bollocks, it's the other way around.

Got my black speckled lounge suit on, nice and baggy, deep pockets. We've been out somewhere, flirting with each other all night long as if we've just met. Pretending we don't know how the other kisses, what her breasts are like, how wet her cunt, how aromatic her arousal.

She looks at me across a crowded disco, blatantly staring at my cunt, Superwoman eyes blazing through lowered lids until my zip melts and my pants catch fire. I am undone and smouldering. She looks up and slightly parts her lips, in her imagination about to bury her face between my legs right then and there, and I have to pretend nothing is happening, carry on trying to order 'two pints of lager and a packet of crisps, please.'

She has on a long black flimsy dress, her outline is barely concealed. Thin straps like welts across a swimmer's shoulders — on a femme such physical strength drives butches wild.

I walk her home, through the parts of King's Cross some call seedy, alley-ways between tenement blocks, badly-lit stamping ground of pros and druggies and all the dregs of society, they say. There is one alley-way in particular, just across from her block. I can see it now, one streetlamp halfway down, long shadows stretching out on either side like a vampire's cloak. I want to sink my teeth into her neck and make her mine. Make her bleed. We approach it, I'm trying to act casual but the bulge in my pants gives me away. Another trophy from Ann Summers, a double dildo I slipped into as I had one last pee before leaving.

I manoeuvre her to the light and pin her to the wall. She can feel what will happen, see it in my eyes. She put the thought there anyway. Lift the hem of her dress, cold brick on her back abrades those muscular shoulders. Kiss her roughly and plunge in. I want to pick her up, thighs around my waist (but I'm not strong enough, tried it once before and we both fell over), clutching her arse in both hands and pulling her open and up. And in my mind's eye I can see a spectator, watching us, seen it all before, pro with her punter and no place to go. I want to walk past, with the light full on our faces, walk past and smile at the realization that we're two women .... When we get in, she'll stand me in the corner of the bedroom, strip me naked, impale me on her fist and turn me gently on my back till I growl and scream and grunt my approval ....

I'm writhing around with myself, wondering what I'm going to do to me next. Do I trust me? Too late for that. The vibrations are going into my arse, bloody hell this is brilliant. Fingers are good — in the right place — but this is ... oh ... uh ... ah ... eh?

Sod's Law. If you buy a vibrator with attachments the only time the fucking top will come off is when it's inside you. It was caught in my vaginal sphincter and the vibrating bottom had come away in my hand. Christ, now what do I do? When something is stuck in a cylindrical container the impulse is to try and approach it from both ends — which is why I found myself with a finger up my bum. No, it wouldn't move. And being well lubricated (sod that last fucking fantasy) it kept slipping out of my grasp. I tried to get in behind it, but panic and a kind of emotional vaginismus meant the muscle clamped onto it like a vice. I was beginning to believe in the vagina dentata.

Now I really was rolling around with myself. I could feel the panic rising in my chest. Please don't let me have to go to hospital, please don't let me be the after-dinner story of some lesbophobic internist.

I was terrified of moving off the bed. Supposing the thing worked itself loose and moved up instead of down? I had visions of lunar modules (same sort of shape) floating in inner space, like Major Tom lost forever in the galactic womb. I was being ridiculous — but you try being cool, calm and collected with an Unidentified Foreign Object up your cunt.

The cat, having sat silently through the whole proceedings, now started screaming to be fed. Usually she purrs nonstop during sexual activity, seemingly fascinated by the comings and goings, sometimes joining in with the surreptitious lick of a nipple — and only disappearing under the bed if I get the whip out. Today she just wants her belly filled. Trying to explain the situation does not help. She screams more and more.

What I really need is a dilator — and then I have a bright idea. Moving very cautiously, one finger up my cunt to keep the thing in place — the irony is killing me — I go into the kitchen. Moggy, thinking it's grub up, does her usual trick of zooming in front, motoring in and out of my feet trying to trip me up like Bullitt on fast-forward. Rooting around in the cutlery drawer confirms her Pavlovian suspicions — that's where 'her' fork is kept. She insinuates herself around my legs. Eventually I find a teaspoon (so that's what 'spooning' means). I don't even bother to hope it will work. Gingerly, I insert it, aware that if my subsiding panic returns I'll be stuck with two UFOs. Cat impatiently tries to manoeuvre me towards the can of Whiskas.

Round the back of the UFO, wishing I had a shoe horn, and the thing suddenly launches itself into infinity with much velocity and a decided plop. It flies through the air, moggy spots it — Okay, one last game before dinner — and dribbles it around the kitchen floor like a feline Maradonna.

I'm dripping with sweat and shaking like a leaf as I dollop the processed horseflesh on her plate. I feel utterly foolish, and the irony of the situation is that I *should* have used a condom. Amazingly, I think to myself, 'I must write to *Spare Rib* and warn other women. "Dear Sisters, A useful trick when using a vibrator is ..."' But would they print it? Another mcp trick to invade women's space and assert the male fantasy that all lesbians use dildoes, vibrators and what have you.

Sorry sisters, but in fact this story is true ....

PARTING GIFT

MINDY MELEYAL

When I look back on the events of yesterday I can scarcely credit them. I'm a pretty quiet type of person and being in a foreign country makes me more so, not less. So how did it happen?

Let me explain. I'm an American student and I've been living in England for a year. When I first came over I guess I wanted a rest from people, some time to think things over before I went back. So I haven't mixed with people much, not even my neighbours, at least not until that crazy day in late July.

I was sitting, as I often did, on my bedroom window-sill, looking down into the yards of the block of student houses where I lived. That day I was watching the two womyn who were preparing to move into a house in the new development opposite. The workmen had just finished so they were clearing builders' rubbish from what would eventually be a garden.

They were good to look at and I was quite content to sit there, the sun beating down on me. I felt like a great big lazy cat half-dreaming, half-watching the two womyn working hard, sweating in the same sunshine, as they shifted the bricks and rubbish from in front of the house. The older one had sun-bleached blond hair, straight, thick and loosely braided, it swung over her shoulders as she bent and stretched rhythmically, throwing things into a dumpster. She was a joy to watch: tanned muscular arms and legs slightly glistening with sweat, muscle shirt and cut-off Levis, dusty and faded. You could tell that if you got close you would be able to see white lines drawn around her (probably) blue eyes and peach-fuzz down on her cheeks. She would occasionally stop and stretch, maybe scratch her back showing the thatches of dark blonde hair under her armpits. I remember thinking, 'Hmmm, a blonde through and through.'

The other, a younger woman, didn't look much more than a girl really. Now, she was something else. She was dark-haired and slight, with translucent white skin indicating summers spent indoors. 'An odd couple,' I thought. The younger one had punky spiked hair and despite the dirty job they were doing was wearing masses of bangles and necklaces and a heavy studded belt over tight black jeans and a cut-off sweatshirt. In her mess of wild black hair there were shocks of pink which echoed her eye make-up. An ill-assorted pair, so obviously unalike, one a left-over hippy, the other a young punk. And yet, even through the distance of my window I could sense an ease between them. They clearly knew each other well: there was no surprise, no edge between them. They worked well together, unspoken understanding, meshed their movements as they systematically cleared the mess left by the workmen.

I smiled at the irony; at last someone was moving into the area that I might be able to talk to, and I was leaving the next day. No matter, I'd come here as much for solitude as for the course I had taken. I sat on the window-sill with little choice. I'd sold nearly all my furniture which had been taken away that morning and my own things were mostly packed and on their way home. So, I sat on my windowsill for want of a chair, and I daydreamed for want of books, music or TV. All I had was a coffee-maker, my hand luggage for the flight and a big bottle of wine left over from the department's end of term party.

My eyes were closing, I felt comfortably stupified by the heat. I was wearing just a loose T-shirt and my underwear, my jeans lay, crumpled, on the floor beside me. The sun was pounding through the window, I could feel little starts of sweat trickling down my back, and I spread my legs to relieve the dampness of my cunt. My fingers were doing nothing in particular, just stroking my thighs, contrasting the burn of their tops with their cool underside in the shade. The soft skin on the underside of my legs was sticky to my touch, and I began idly running my hands up and down then trailing long, lazy spirals as I dreamed. The sun was hot, reminding me of home and childhood, a time when I felt free to enjoy my body without adult prohibitions on what I should or should not do.

I smiled for no one but myself as I noticed that my right hand toyed idly with the elastic of my underwear, producing a gentle and rhythmic pull on my cunt. 'Why not?' I thought. 'It's my body and no one can see.' All the other apartments were empty, eveyone had gone except the two womyn toiling in the yard opposite, and they were too engrossed in their own labours to notice me.

I don't get noticed much, never have. I stand on the edge of people's lives usually. Edge, ledge, shelf (my family's word for my position), and now a window-sill. 'What a place to wank!' I thought, and looked around to see if God or anybody had noticed me thinking such disgraceful thoughts right out there in the open. No, nobody noticed. And what if they did? Could I be deported? Would they withhold my degree? Make me do it again on TV AM? I lingered on that last notion and shuffled into a more comfortable position.

My fingers slid under the pink polka-dots of my underwear, finding the contrast between smooth thigh and tangle of pubic hair as much of a surprise as ever.

'Grass sure grows well on quiet streets,' I thought, reflecting on my year of solitude. 'Oh go on, spoil yourself.'

I paused to breathe in the smell on my fingers and have another good mouthful of wine. Mercifully it was stood in a patch of shade and remainded quite cool. I licked my fingers reflectively and slid my other hand under my T-shirt to hold my breast as my cunt beckoned irresistibly. I pulled my legs up and spread my knees so my hand fell easily over my cunt and I stroked it, feeling the heat even through my underwear. Almost imperceptibly my fingers sidled over and around the pink polka-dots, found the elastic at the leg and snuck in under it, trespassing, it seemed, by their stealth. They brushed my pubic hair and I squirmed to meet them; they were teasing and sly as they woke my body from its long slumber. I began to feel that delicious tingle and looked once again at the two womyn in the yard. Yes, they were too engrossed to take any notice of me, so I settled down to enjoy myself. My fingers circled and probed, sinking into my cunt and slowly pulling out. Sliding up to my clit, and round, and then away, and back to my cunt. At first just one finger and then as my juices began to flow, two, then three, until my cunt was wide open and I could flex and curl all my fingers in the liquid warmth. I was really getting into it all: the sunshine, my exposed position on the window-sill, the wine and my impending orgasm. I could feel my clit harden, standing out from my lips when I realised that something had changed outside.

All the heat had gone out of the day, and the awful English weather was asserting itself again. The sky was leaden, purple and threatening. I stopped and looked out of the window as the skies opened and raindrops fell like coins thudding onto the dry earth, the sidewalk and the womyn. I could see the rain washing dust in rivers down them, clinging clothes to their suddenly still bodies. They were looking at each other, startled, the cloudburst had taken them too by surprise.

It was obvious that the rain was here to stay and I smiled to think that I would leave England as I found it, sodden. The sun-baked blonde shrugged at the yard and the heavens above it; their day's labour was clearly at an end, and as she did so the younger one bent down quickly to the puddled earth, scooped up a handful of mud and clapped it right on the other's breast, smearing finger-trails all over her body. The response was prompt, within seconds they were laughing and hurling the wet soil at each other until the young punk's hair was dowsed in a cascade of mud. They were nearly indistinguishable, apart from the older womon's braids which hung like wet ropes down to her breasts. And then they were kissing! Right out there in front of God and everyone!

The rain came down harder until they were both running with water. The yard had become a series of small lakes with raindrops bouncing in and out of them. I couldn't take my eyes off the two womyn and I slowly became aware that they were looking straight up at me. They looked at each other, then back at me, and then they both smiled, beckoning. Nothing in my mid-western upbringing had prepared me for this kind of social event but I didn't need to be told what to do. I grabbed the wine as I jumped off the window-sill and headed straight downstairs to the yard where the womyn were waiting for me. I shivered as the rain, or the enormity of what I was about to enjoy engulfed me. Was I really going to do this? Make love with two totally unfamiliar womyn, in a yard, in the rain?

The hell I was! Chances like this don't come in pairs. I just hoped I wasn't hallucinating the whole thing. I opened the gate into their yard and put down the wine bottle.

Their arms encircled me and it felt so good after these months of solitude, womyn's arms around me, breasts pressing against mine. And the kisses, all mud and sweat and rain, tongues in my ears, on my neck. And hands, hands everywhere. I soaked it in, the plants in the parched garden were not more grateful than I. The long drought was over, I was loved and replenished. Together we sank to the ground. 'Mother Nature is wonderful,' I thought, as the two womyn enfolded and caressed me.

I was just about to speak when the older womon put her finger to my lips and silenced me, as the younger slithered down my body, kissing me and placing her own fingers where, minutes earlier, mine had given me such pleasure. A rain-soaked braid fell across me as I kissed a mud-smeared mouth. Somehow my hand found a breast which was full, soft and rounded. We scarcely noted the whistling of the paper boy who passed by, oblivious to our presence, merged as we were with the good earth. As he faded into the next court we exchanged glances and got to our feet unsteadily, supporting each other, unwilling to break the contact we had made. The younger womon picked up the wine bottle, we drank, and in silent assent crossed back to my house.

We trailed mud over silent, cool-tiled floors, leaving a pattern of intermingled footprints to mark our direction. We reached the bathroom and peeled sodden clothing from each other's bodies. Together we stood in the tub and sluiced away the remains of the garden, revealing as we did skin patterned by sun and hystory. A belly wrinkled in childbearing, a knee awkwardly scarred, a neat appendectomy. We paused in appreciation of our beauty and our intentions.

And so, to bed. We kissed, and held, and loved our mutual womonness. Breasts and bellies, arms and necks, we merged into each other. Slow, so slow, fingers trailing ripples of desire up thighs. Cunts opening like water lilies. Our skins seemed to unite, inside, outside, you, me, her, all are one. My tongue encircled a clit, and my own cunt felt the burn. A hand brushed my breast and another voice gasped with delight.

They seemed to sense my need for fingertips, tongue, breast, my lust for simple flesh against flesh. As the younger gave herself to the space between my legs the older knelt astride me, offering her cunt to my mouth, her breasts to my hands as she stroked my hair. My tongue moved as her tongue moved, desire eddied around us, enfolding and enmeshing us. Fingers filled my cunt as my tongue found haven. My cries as I came were drowned in a cunt so soft and inviting, then urgent, demanding. My fingers were guided then to another place of delight, smaller but still welcoming. A hand joined mine caressing breasts which swung ripe and heavy over me. Inside, outside, you, me, her, she, we, womyn, bellies, breasts, fingers, tongues and cunts feasting each other.

The storm subsided, the pounding rain paused and stopped. All was quiet and the smell of fresh, damp earth outside rose to the tang of cunts inside. The evening grew dim and still. I rolled a joint and we shared it, the match flare illuminating our faces. It wasn't clear who started it, but first we smiled, then giggled, and laughed right out loud: audacity and love so intermingled.

'Well,' said the younger, 'we won't get the garden finished today, will we Mum?'

NEVER BEFORE

NINA RAPI

Like a bitch on heat
you satisfied yourself
on my willing thigh

so urgent so intense
more out of necessity   your pain to relieve me
and less out of lust   to do it with me

Your eyes bewildered
my eyes just wondering
how come you do this
so freely
What changed you so   Mother!

Another Mother, friend of yours
was similarly wetting her daughter's thigh

You both had the duty of
sick people to look after
in dark, remote caves
surrounded by the sea

We, the daughters, visitors
were to heal you
were to give you strength
to carry on or
help you to escape

Mother, I never had
this dream before

A VISIT TO THE HAIRDRESSER

CUNTESSA DE MONS VENERIS

I am six. I am standing in the doorway to my grandma's bedroom. My mother is sitting in my grandma's big bed nursing my brother. His eyes are closed as he sucks and sucks. One tiny hand clasps her breast. The colour of my mother's skin is warm brown. She rocks my brother gently. Suddenly I feel a surge of intense jealousy. I want to curl up in her lap, and take her hard dark brown nipple in my mouth, and drink her milk. I tiptoe to the edge of the bed and get in. She smiles at me and caresses my head. I touch her breast. She tells me to sit still. I ask if I can suck her breast. She says no. Sharply. Then she says gently, that I'm too old for that sort of thing. I want to cry, but I suck my thumb instead, and sulk.

I am sitting flipping through the pages of a Black hair fashion magazine, in the waiting room of my hairdresser. None of the women have natural hair. All the women in the adverts have been made up and photographed to look as European as possible. I fiddle with my dreads. Surrounding me are rows of hair conditioners, oils, curl activators and shampoos. Styrotex dummies heads, looking like macabre death masks are covered with all colours of wigs from jet black to platinum blonde! I finger my locks which suddenly feel dry and out of condition. I hope the hairdresser does not start to lecture me about that. The pungent, unpleasant, sickly smell of hair being straightened drifts through from the salon. The receptionist smiles at me with her full purple lips. Her curly perm glitters under the lights. She tells me to go upstairs for Sylvia to wash my hair.

The room is empty, except for four white basins in a row. Four gaping mouths, ready for someone's neck to be placed in their little crooks. Beside each basin are groups of identical bottles. In front of each hard shiny basin is a chair with white padded seats, and chrome armrests. The white walls reflect the fluorescent lights harshly. They make my eyes hurt.

A door at the end of the room opens and Sylvia comes towards me, plump red towels draped over her arms. She stuffs them around my neck. They are warm like her breath on my face. I sit in one of the chairs, and sink my neck into one of the grooves of the basins. Sylvia selects a tape, puts it into the cassette recorder, then bends over me to turn on the taps. Her ripe mango breasts, brush lightly against my cheek. I close my eyes and listen to the music. She wets my hair, then applies the shampoo, running her fingers on my scalp.

Gently, slowly, in circles
Gently, slowly, in circles
She massages my head ....
Her nipples brush against my lips.
My heart beats in time to the music.
Thump. Thump. My heart.
The music.

As she rinses my hair it makes little squeaky noises when she squeezes the water out. I lick a nipple through her blouse. I nibble a nipple. She squeezes the water out of my locks. Her nipple hardens. I undo her blouse, one button at a time. I lift her breasts to my mouth and sink my teeth into their full firmness, into her nipples.

Harder and harder.
Her taste is sharp.

131

She presses her body
Onto mine, harder and harder
I bite her nipples. She cries out. In pain?

... I'm not sure. The sound of my heart echoes in my ears, I can no longer hear the music. Has it stopped? The water is still gushing and hissing on my hair. Suddenly I am aware of her perfume — woody and mossy.

She finishes rinsing my hair and rings my locks. She sinks her face into my neck, caressing it with her lips. I can hear the music again. Her body is still moulded to mine. I want to pinch her nipples hard for scaring me like that. Instead I push her down between my legs to her knees. She rubs her naked breasts up and down my thigh. Then she takes my hand and encircles each finger with her hot, wet tongue. Lovingly. She pulls the silk scarf from around her neck and rubs it over my face. It is cool and smooth. She rubs it onto her soft, floppy breasts and passes it between her legs, then hands it to me.

'Get up and bend over that basin.'

I tie each of her wrists to the taps, then ease her skirt up gently and pull her pants down.

'Spread your legs wider.'

Her damp, sweet, sweat, heat rises from between her thighs. My thumb strokes her chrysanthemum arsehole. The petals open as she relaxes and lets me in. Sylvia moans and croons and sways to the music.

She moans and sways

'Fuck me'

To the music

'Fuck me' she whispers.

'Fuck me.'

I whip her round buttocks. They quiver in slow motion and ripple to the sound of each smack. I rub them firmly. The juices from her pussy trickle down her full plump thighs. Through her silky pubic hairs I see her long dark-red lips; fleshy and swollen. My fingers slide over that so wet kiss to her long hard clit. She shudders and pushes down on my hand. Sylvia. Sylvia. I slip two fingers into her slit.

I dive into her cunt.

Her folded walls hug me.

I resurface

Then dive into her juices again.

'Please do it harder,' she begs.

Fuck me

Harder.

First two fingers, then three, then four. Now my whole hand. She wants them all. We are rocking slowly at first. Slowly my fist pushes inside her. Then faster and faster. She gyrates her hips round my hand. Harder and harder. We are rocking, bucking, fucking together.

'Yes'

Fucking

'Y..e...s'

Rocking

'Y..E..S'

Bucking

'FUCK ME YOU BASTARD'

She lets out a loud sigh and collapses against the sink. Her body looks so soft and hot and vulnerable against the hard white ceramic. Sweat is pouring down the back of her neck. It is all so strange and silent, then she starts to laugh. I untie her wrists and find myself laughing too. I rub them gently where the scarf has left a mark. She gets up and we hold each other, hips grinding to the music.

'I'm going to put the conditioner in, then you can get under the steamer.'

I open my eyes. Through a gap in her blouse where the buttons meet I can see little beads of perspiration on her breasts. I can feel a tightness in my cunt. I know I am wet. She smiles at me and takes my towels away, and I feel her warm breath on my face.

VICKI AND DAPHNE

CHERYL CLARKE

Being given a lover's key is an intimate gesture:
without it one can figure what course the relationship
will take; with it, trust is a temptation.

Blood of the cut from a serrated knife
blotted by a slice of cake, frosted white
and garnished with a sugar-molded rose
the same color red as her blood
set Vicki to musing on the risk she'd taken
coming from an office party without warning
with half a cake to persuade Daphne.

No bandages in Daphne's medicine cabinet
or night table. (Daphne never had what Vicki
needed when she needed it. But Vicki was an
ex-Marine and compensated by being relentlessly
adaptable.) So, she scissored a sanitary pad
down to the size of a Curad (to her amazement
Daph did have pads) and taped it round her
haemorrhaging finger with Daph's last bit of
scotch tape.

Vicki's feet hurt in her business pumps.
Her business suit pinched her waist and pressed
her breasts. The scent of perfume and deodorant
mixed with the odor emanating from her pits.
She didn't want to get too comfortable. She

preferred to await Daphne's pleasure. Her feet
might swell or Daph might want her to book.

Vicki removes one shoe and slides the other off
her burning heel. (She carries sneakers in her
bag but can't really stand the way treads look
with nylons.)
All day she'd been driven by lust for Daphne. She'd
left messages by everyone who might see or speak to
Daph to tell her she wanted her.

Where is Daphne? Surely she'd be home soon so
Vicki could take off her clothes and complain
about her aching pussy.

Being in Daphne's apartment at 11 pm without
warning and Daphne not home but imminent,
fantasy o'ertakes Vicki. The sound of Daph's
keys in both holes
turning noisily
the house dark
Daphne comes for Vicki where she sits
runs her hand along her nylons
and beyond
Vicki guides her hand.

Her throbbing finger draws her back to
the reality of her situation: fully
clothed, horny, and without
warning and how would she be able to take
Daph up the cunt with her middle finger
bandaged bulkily?
She couldn't even stand air on the wound.
Could she Daphne's salty cunt?
And her right hand was not so dextrous.

136

Does Daphne come? Vicki prepares an
appropriately humble expression and
the honest explanation: *Baby, I'm gonna
keep on lovin you til the day I die,
cuz I love the way you satisfy.**
No keys in holes.
No Daphne.
Only next door neighbor fumbling.
Without warning, Vicki feels cramps.
Her ankles swell. Her finger bleeds every
time she flexes. Her pussy is gamey with
secretions. She wants to lie down. But
Daph hates wrinkled bed clothes.

Vicki falls into a daze, limps to Daph's bed
and pulls back its comforter and top sheet
limps then to an odd chest of drawers
and removes a small object of comfort.
After pulling her skirt to her crotch,
lies face down on Daph's bed
and applies it to her genitals
eleven times
calling Daph a whore sweetly
and being Daph calling herself a
bitch roughly.
Vicki sleeps deeply in suit, nylons,
and one pump, awaking at 6 am
without warning, without Daphne
returns the object to its place
pulls top sheet and comforter
over passion and menses stained sheets
smooths her wrinkles
brushes the lint.

*Sung by B.B. King

BACK TRACKING

FIFI

Arlene cast her eyes across the newly cleaned livingroom. All her papers, letters, old magazines and bills to pay and bills paid neatly filed away in their just-created filing system. A sense of satisfaction crept through her, made her feel good and at ease with herself. Only it was hot; stuffy, still heat that wouldn't go away no matter how many different windows she opened, no matter how many doors she opened.

It was early evening, Sunday evening. Outside nothing was happening. No one seemed to be doing anything, only the distant voices of children playing, screaming and shouting at each other. Arlene wondered what to do with herself. A restlessness took over from her earlier feelings of achievement and ease with herself. The heat was beginning to get to her. Irritability took over from restlessness. Why is it so hot? Why won't the air move? Instead of giving in to restlessness and dissatisfaction, Arlene decided to treat herself for all her hard work that day. Treat herself because it was back to work the next day. She picked up her jangle of keys, video membership card and some money left on the mantlepiece.

She bought vanilla ice-cream, strawberries, a half bottle of brandy, Perrier and some chocolate. Next stop, video shop. Arlene was trying to avoid asking herself why she always got so nervous before she went into the video shop. She'd been in loads of times; had successfully negotiated not paying for overdue videos and it wasn't exactly a porn video shop. She thought about it briefly: maybe it was because she never knew which video to get out, always had to ask what was around; maybe it was because she liked the look of the woman who worked there.

The woman always wore her hair neatly groomed and close cut. Her tight curls neatly trimmed, without a trace of activator. She looked mean, but always had a kind-of-smile on her face. She always dressed casual, always wore jeans and something: jeans and T-shirt; jeans and shirt; jeans and sweatshirt — depending on what the weather was doing. Today it was jeans and T-shirt.

Arlene did not think of her as a stereotype butch, but she couldn't help but notice the tattoo peeking out from the short sleeve, the heavy gold rings she wore on her fingers, and her neatly clipped nails.

Arlene looked at her T-shirt, but all she saw was the woman's large, firm breasts, nipples teasing through the cotton, muscular arms and broad shoulders. Her eyes slid down the woman's body and rested on her full crotch and arse. Tightly packed into 501s, Arlene wanted to run her hands over ... enough of that Arlene.

Now which video? Scanning her eyes over the top row, Arlene couldn't see anything that grabbed her. She'd seen all the half-decent sex films, besides she didn't want a sex video. She fancied some dreamy romance, some bullshit film of boy meets girl with good photography, interesting angles and easy storyline.

'What're you looking for?'

'Oh, anything really. Well, nothing violent, nothing scary. You know, just some easy story. Recommend anything?'

'This one's just come in. It's kind of like 'Love Story II', but it's got an interesting twist to it. Try it. And no, she doesn't get leukemia!'

Arlene sceptically but eagerly looked over the jacket. It seemed to be just what she was in the mood for. She glanced up at the woman and caught her serious, brown eyes staring down at her. Arlene looked back at the jacket nervously, quickly.

'Mm, might as well try it.' She cracked a smile.

Her sweaty hands had worked through the tissue paper on the brandy, juggling the goodies around she managed to find the right key. Home.

Getting herself set up didn't take long. Arlene decided to keep the ice-cream for later. Brandy was all she wanted, with lots of ice. She stripped herself down to vest and knickers. It was still too hot, but Arlene was feeling shy. Besides who really does sit on their own in the stifling evening heat with absolutely no clothes on? Common decency, keep the vest and knickers on, Arlene.

The video set. Arlene settled into the floor cushions, made herself comfy despite the heat, sipped slowly at her brandy. The video started playing. Just beyond arm's reach, the remote. Shit. Arlene stretched over, grabbed it. Fast foward through the trailers. Why did the music always sound the same in these videos? It always sounds the same.

The brandy seeped into her system; the ice cooled her throat, she played with the glass, pressing it against her thighs, her cheeks, her neck. She watched the video, not really paying any mind to the actual story, she didn't need to anyway. She just watched the images on the screen, unconsciously looking harder as the seduction scene approached ...

They'd been falling over each other at the office all day, bumping into each other, her dropping papers all over the floor, both avoiding eye contact with each other but forcing each other to catch glances, eyes. Eventually they had their date and it was back to hers for coffee. She was standing in the kitchen waiting for the coffee, waiting to be kissed, wanting to be moved against by that hard but gentle body ....

Arlene was always interested in sex, sex scenes. She could feel herself soften, widen out. Her mind not thinking; her body just feeling relaxed and open. Arlene moved her hands over her soft, dark thighs, moved them over her even-softer belly. Without thinking her arm moved between her legs, pressed against her cunt. Moved up and into her aching cunt, dragging her knickers up, pulling between her legs. Her head thrown back against the sofa, eyes closed and not thinking about her actions.

'That's how I want you. Keep moving. Make yourself comfortable. I want to see you.'

Arlene didn't look up to see where the vaguely familiar voice was coming from. She carried on. Moving against the cushion. Feeling her knickers tighten against her. Rubbing herself against herself, she continued.

'Take your pants off. Show me yourself. I'm only going to watch you. Come on! Show me yourself!'

Arlene lifted her arse off the cushion, pushed her pants off. Slipped them off her smooth, dark legs. Her strong legs opened. Let loose into the hot air the smell of her cunt. Open wide, her legs fixed themselves either side of the cushion.

'Move inside yourself. I want to see you enter yourself. Uh, uh, no, not just one finger. Push yourself for me, ease into yourself. I want to see your cunt open up for you.'

Arlene wanted to feel her breasts. Her nipples were taut, erect. Rubbing against her vest. Tingling against the feel of cotton. As she pushed her fingers into her cunt she felt the wetness suck her fingers in. No more pushing. Her fingers eased in. Her thumb pressed against her clitoris. She massaged her whole cunt. Felt the firm clitoris resist the advances of her thumb. Wanting more pressure she began to move deeper inside herself. For some reason Arlene opened her eyes. She looked up at the video.

Staring at her boldly, leaning forward as if to get a better view, was her lady from the video shop, watching her. She was wearing the same smile she always wore, but now it seemed deeper and more like a lecherous grin. She leaned forward to whisper,

'Don't ask me a thing. I'm watching you, don't stop. I want to see you fuck yourself. Go on, for me!'

Arlene felt a rush through her body, she couldn't quite understand what exactly was going on. A twinge of curiosity threatened to voice itself, but the rush pulled Arlene back and deeper into herself. She moved to greet her hand and expose herself even more.

Deeper Arlene moved into herself, harder she fucked herself. Her smell filled her nose. She could smell her sex fill the room's still, warm air. She slowed down. Opened her eyes to see a face enraptured with the vision of her cunt, excitedly, anxiously awaiting confirmation of what she was anticipating, waiting for, watching for.

Moving inside herself Arlene could feel her orgasm coming. She kept calling for her woman to keep watching her, crying out into the quiet evening, begging for this woman to see her coming.

She felt her cunt clutching her fingers, holding on stronger and stronger. Arlene's response was to push deeper and deeper.

As she came down from her orgasm she heard a voice reassuring her, comforting her,

'Good girl, well done. You are a beautiful woman. I liked that a lot.'

Arlene lifted her hair to cool her neck, lay her head against the sofa, her eyes closed. She concentrated on breathing deeply, reached for the brandy, cooled her face and sipped slowly.

A glance up at the video told her that her lovestruck couple had only just made it to the second kiss. Arlene smiled, reached for the remote. Rewind. Sat back to enjoy the video.

CROSS-QUESTION

TERRI JEWELL

somebody said
coz i'm no
      straight
      white boy
i got a triple dip pain
as if hate
      stops in three's
as if i make the claim
but rest assured
that somebody ain't seen
      the power in my arm
           ain't smelled
      my love come down
           ain't heard
      a black dyke's song

CONFESSIN'

STORME WEBBER

yes, is true i confess ... continued source of inspiration n all that. what has always been smoothest & most continually satisfying in my life. also of course most complicated. women, oh the agony the ecstasy. those things that just happen to my body sometime when one of em looks, smiles or speaks a certain way at me ... a deep earth vibration & all the elements in various combination fire/water/air/earth reforming and ascending as new and different stronger entities. all of this magic can i feel when she look at me that kinda way/ like all the sudden we could be somewhere else/close/tremblin heart to heart/ & she look at me that way/ from under her eyelid/ & my heart has a small attack/ reconsiders/decides to live on for the delicious future ... the truth in the touch the taste, the space we sculpt into a new construct (more room to grow in, more room to grow in) and peel away everything, throw the masks aside some/ i want you not your image/ flesh blood sweat/ not politeness not social convention/ not a glimpse, but a whole flash blast of pure funky love.

POEM FOR A DIVA

STORME WEBBER

big strong women
wit fierce attitude in the street
an exquisitely arched eyebrow
may be/ all she has/ for you
but she got something else to show me
behind that worldly camouflage
we was soft-to-soft
rock & water & earth shuddered
rose & fell
and that fierce strong woman
cried sweet sacred tears
i had no answer for
except to hold her
tighter.

MISH-MISH RIMON

L.A. LEVY

We are desired in bars. I feel us trapped in the gaze of someone I can, or cannot see. Sometimes she will come over and say,

'What are you? Spanish, Italian, Greek?'

'What are you talking about? You seem so animated.'

We are sometimes thought to be beautiful, our faces reminiscent of other times, other places. Something old in our eyes, in the way our limbs lie upon each other as we sit.

To some, we are amusingly ugly. To most we are all white.

What is it about us that the Goyim can't quite put their finger on?

My lover and I are both jews. She is an ashkenazi and sometimes fits the image of the typical Eastern European. A Sheyne Meydel, she cooks, she plutzes. I am a first cousin to the beigal and anxiety culture; I am mixed and my family is proud to be Persian.

So we are Jewesses, and our image troubles us: more ethnic, more sexy. We have a reputation among the Goyim for being very free ... tempered of course with stereoptypical Jewish angst.

As for the good Jewish girl, we know she keeps kosher, she brings up her kids right, she is wild betweeen the sheets on Friday night, but when I asked the Rabbi's wife,

'What do I have? What do we get?'

The only answer she had for a Jewish lesbian was,

'Come to my home. I will talk with you and show you how to be a good Jewish woman.'

And she wasn't offering excitement. Re-education was on the menu.

Do we have Jewish sex?

We have our memories and our histories. My parents had sex. They had that particular closeness. Friday night and my mother would dress up: her perfume, her jewels, it was a mitzvah.

And I remember my mother, single in the 60s, going out at weekends. Her red blouse. I remember her breasts, her perfume. Women had hair in those days, big and bright and high and thick. Her black pants, her heels. Her boyfriends were cab drivers, car dealers. Cocky men, flashy, with East End and West End accents. She always told me about them and what happened after the cups of coffee.

My mother tried to be the epitome of Good English Taste. You had to fit in.

As she got older we had the Jewish Divorced and Separated scene. Weekly meeting at a tasteful and discreet venue. The men were charming, a bit shabby and desperate. If a woman could overcome her distaste, she could find a nice cultured man, or perhaps someone to mother. The women all seemed very nice, very clever, very attractive, but they all had pisks, they knew how to bitch, those women.

We had our fantasies.

I wanted to seduce the Rabbi's son on one of our Sunday walks in the park. Those clever boys with sensuous lips and long pale fingers.

I would be your flash Jew boy boyfriend, pick you up in the car, sweet talk you.

I would sit across from you in the synagogue, seduce you with my eyes.

We could eye each other with maximum intensity as we turn the pages of our siddurs.

We could be biblical lovers. I could lie between your breasts all day. You would feed me fruit, grapes and wine. I'd take everything from your fingertips. But we are in diaspora baby, and we have to live in the world.

To live in the world is hard enough, but bubeleh, to live in the world as a Jew! How to live a talmudic life, a cabbalistic life in diasporan chaos? A rule for everything we have and we have our duties and even a woman has her rights. My mother's right to my father as her lover, to be loved sweetly. Fucking is supposed to be a pleasure, and pleasure is to be shared. And if he's no good? She can throw him out. She can drag him to the Rabbi for an emotional scene, she can make her accusations.

Rituals to mark us out. Circumcision! It's a regular issue in a big family. Always a lot of nice parties and never being able to see from the back of the crowd. Explaining why I was taking the day off to my friends at school was no joke.

When I had my first period we knew we had to be traditional.

'Come and slap my face!' I shouted from the toilet.

My mother slapped my face gently and we laughed and opened a bottle of wine. I was now a woman. Was it for my future shame? Had I become knowing? Some of these customs mystify me.

Sex and life and kashrut and shul. We don't believe in Good/Evil, body/soul. We express ourselves with our whole bodies, we are beautiful when we talk. We know that sex and life and kashrut and shul aren't separate. Love and intellect, there is no cut off. Sex also belongs to our minds. So many sexy intellectual Jews. We are an oral tradition (do we do a lot of oral sex?).

We write poetry, we respect our past. We read the Song of Songs and we know it's about a Persian and a cool intellectual Ethiopian. We are into being sexy. We like to dress up. Those women in my family — you never see big English women in tight shiny sheath dresses having a wild time at weddings. Women with heap-of-wheat bellies and hairy legs, lips beautiful with dark moustaches. We know how to celebrate.

We have our past and how brilliant we are at remembering, but the present, we are lousy at dealing with, and the future?

From past to future if we know the roots of our sex.

We are lovers, we are Jews and both women. Do we have Jewish sex?

We could be two Jewish anarchists. Intellectual but passionate, clever but taking a few too many risks. Marxists completely cool and brainy. We are radicals having urgent sex after the meeting. I watch your fingers leafing through sheets of paper, see you lift your spectacles on your big Jewish nose. We read everything and we breathe our knowledge in smokey rooms. Our eyes meet as we argue a bitter point and we are turned on by the struggle. Later we will want each other, devour each other with big open mouths. Tear off each other's clothes and hold on to each other and fuck. Pulling each other round corners in the city streets, embracing in doorways. We know we have no time to lose. We will struggle and like partisans, we would fight many battles.

A frum couple in the suburbs. You come from work and the dinner is ready. We have Friday night, it's never as mystical as film shabbas, with the semi-darkness and mournful prayer. Momma in the lace head-cover and Poppa, quiet and intense, reading his way fluently through the prayer book.

You watch me light candles and your eyes fill with tears as you remember your own mother. A saint! My body is round and sweet and you sit in the chair with the posture of a Jew, a man who must sell everything. What rhythm must have developed between us, if we had led a talmudic life-style! A rule for everything ... much of our communication is silent, we have a thousand faces, a thousand gestures. You pass me the salt and I am overcome with desire. So we make love. Because we are completely intimate and completely intense and because it's a mitzvah.

Or we could be Hebrew Biblical Poetry lovers. I'd make you Queen Esther. Take you to your long mirror and dress you in silks, purple and gold. Braid your hair, oiled and combed with perfume. Spices at your wrists. Paint kohl onto your eyes, lift your hair, kiss your neck. Slide my hands over your waist, lift the silk over your thighs, catch the hairs on your legs. Kiss your ear. Reach down over your sweet, long hairs, curled and damp, catch the edge of your lips, slide my fingers into your cunt, fuck you. Press pomegranate to your lips, say 'suck' with my hand, find your breast — like fruits, your nipples like rubies, sweet and hard. Reach down under your silk, with my tongue, taste you,a thousand delicious juices on my tongue, spices and wine and fuck you my darling, gazelle.

We could be Woody Allen lovers, have a scenario of complete desperation and awkwardness: you a New York intellectual, me a hopeless inept classical musician suffering a crisis of confidence. I invite you to my place for dinner and in my attempt to demonstrate my considerable Jewish homemaking skills succeed in ruining the dinner, nearly electrocuting myself on the fridge and blowing the fuse circuit while tripping up on the standard lamp wire, which is trailing across the doorway as I enter the room with the coffee which I spill whilst falling at your feet, and somehow, I'm down there, energetically apologizing and the next moment we are staring into each other's eyes. Moving towards each other, lips leading the way. So we fall passionately onto the floor and have the most wild sex rolling around and squeezing our hips into each other, coming against each other's thighs whilst simultaneously tearing off each other's jeans and trying to fuck each other. At which point almost everything on tables and shelves is on the floor and frustration with clothes is mounting, so we run into the bedroom hand-in-hand, out of breath and red-faced and we are hit, suddenly, by the most incredible shyness: we are passionate but sensitive. So we make love, and in the morning we are, of course, embarrassed, but we know we share something.

Can we objectify each other? We have been accused of exoticising each other.

My lover and I are both Jews, so we don't have that body/mind split. We take from the past and we know the importance of memory. We re-make our future in our fantasy.

We could dream anything up.

ONE NIGHT REUNION

TERRI JEWELL

she smoked a cigarette
   while i chatted in lavendar
                 sleepiness,
our hunched shoulders
   touching like the good
                 friends
      we were .....
fourteen once more
   and close in the moist
                curves
      of the other's memory -
chasing summer with bare thighs
necking under tenement stairs
shaking trees for snow
kicking bottles in midnight lots
     and being oh so bold
     with our stark glances,
it all came back ....
we tossed wildly in waves rolling
   from hair to fingers
      teeth and breasts
it has been awhile, she said.
it has been awhile, i echoed.

A PERFECT STRANGER

FIONA COOPER

Jay landed in the middle of a champagne dyke birthday party, and let the niagara of innuendo soothe her soul. Then all the tough rangy women hit the street, leaving her with Tim and Wainwright, and a perfect stranger called Sally. Who sparkled and looked wonderful as she wove stories as outrageous as they were funny, Madeline Kahn and Lily Tomlin in every gesture. And when she was listening she looked like herself: a nice, sweet self.

They swapped movie stories. Jay lit Sally's cigarette.

'Since I'm flirting with you anyway,' she said, feeling easy.

Sally smiled, like *of course you're flirting with me*. Not too surprised, but pleased all the same.

'She's nice,' Jay told Tim at the bar.

'How are *you?*' he said, 'You looked shell-shocked earlier. You should smile more. Sally's marvellous. You're blossoming.'

And so she blossomed, bloomed, exuded radiance to Sally. She began to feel good. GODDAMMIT! She felt good. They persuaded Sally to stay and drink sherry, preparing herself for a very New England visit with the folks. Finally, Sally left.

'To hell with it,' said Jay, 'I'll give her a ring. I want to see her. Tim, you said she lives near you — I'll give you a ride home.'

'Good, — I've got to find Wainwright, he's pissed — we've got to pick up a dead pigeon from Sally's front door anyway ...'

Dead pigeon? Jay giggled, remembering Sally's B-movie horror at finding it.

Wainright emerged, pale and draped over Tim's shoulder, full of the sort of apologies people make when they're very, very drunk. Neither Jay nor Tim gave a damn. Wainright kept saying: 'Drop us here, Jay, it's okay.'

'I'm taking you right to the door,' said Jay. 'You do have Sally's address, eh Tim?'

Tim grinned like a pixie.

The boys moved the pigeon and said goodnight, and Sally said to Jay, 'Come in.'

They sat and talked for a while. Both having troubles, both a little bruised, both needing some love. Sally was quieter with only Jay as audience, sweetly self-mocking with a lingering smile and an easy dirty laugh. Jay relaxed and found her cowboy sense of humour again — so long unused in the serious years with Elizabeth, the tension and pain of Lucy.

So then Jay said, 'I want to sleep with you.'

Sally smiled and nodded, like *of course you do*, and said,

'Well, let's go to bed.'

(Is life ever this refreshingly simple? Yes.)

'Really?' said Jay.

'Really,' said Sally, brushing the ash from her cigarette and smiling.

Goddammit, thought Jay, she's really pleased.

And they kissed, just to make sure it was the best idea they'd had all evening. Sally had a lovely mouth — Jay had been watching her talk and smoke, wisecrack and drink all evening. Lovely lips, lovely smile, lovely eyes the way the sea is glorious as it breaks on golden sand. Her skin was golden.

And probably is still, thought Jay, in the heart of the country, luxuriating in the memories. Lovely Sally, lashings of style and a million dollar smile.

Write you a letter, Sally, and this is what it says.

Oh god, thought Jay, closing her eyes for a rhapsody of sheer pleasure.

Your tongue was wet and warm on my lips, my mouth, our lips clinging, brushing, nuzzling deep into our hungry, starving, greedy, needy mouths. You traced my cheek with your tongue, my mouth moved on your smooth neck, tongue stroking behind your ear, your earlobe between my lips. Athletic tongues working out. A handclasp ....

'Well, let's go to bed,' you said.

I peed, you peed. You brushed your teeth, I heard, and tasted a moment later. I was touched. You poured the last of your brandy into two glasses and rolled a cigarette.

'Dregs!' you said, laughing, like I-don't-believe-this, honey.

Not your style to one-night stand. Not mine.

You held me close, closer, I held you. You're about my height, Sally, a nice size for a woman like me holding you. I unzipped your dress — with my bare hands. Oh, how I love that moment: clothes shuck away, and our breasts touch, navels touch, your thighs pressed against mine against yours. I felt the heat and the bone and the soft spring turf of golden hair, registered the hot touch of you ... suddenly, I know my twin from inside.

Yeah, thought Jay, twins. They twin towns: I've passed through a dozen today, Mogadon-on-the-Ooze twinned with Les Neiges d'Antan ... and I am the remote hamlet of Thrilling Springs, high on a fir-treed hill, and you, oh Sally, you are La Belle Inconnue.

So we were swaying there, my fingertips ruffled the bleached gold fur so hot on my thigh, the edge of your bed conspiring with my knees to knock me off my feet; your hand moved down my body, like checking — you know? Tantalizing. You swung onto your bed and we knelt like two Sumo wrestlers stoned out of their brains, swaying and hypnotised and whatever next?

Jay grinned and poured more wine. The sun was burning off the mists and soon she'd go walking in a breeze to blow her mind. Whatever next?

Your thigh between mine between yours and I got to know your shoulder's smooth exciting pulse; your arms around me and mine the same and we looked at each other and laughed. Slow and gentle and reee-aally silly, Sally. Like — delighted.

You knew, I knew you knew and on and on. Sally, you have lovely eyelashes and your hands are thrilling. You stroked my neck, wrapped your silky legs around me and ...

'I wish you were here right now!' said Jay aloud, 'More wine!'

The volcano of my navel erupted, a lava flow of pure desire flowed through the fabulously invaded mountain fastness of Thrilling Springs! Oh, yeah! My hand took a sleigh-ride along your thighs and one by one my fingers went waltzing into the steamy Florida swamp where rare and magic flowers grow, and your sweet face shivered like a broken reflection and you gasped, I gasped, as your body burst into bloom.

Oh, Sally, my hand was too far away, I slalomed my face to the cornsilk of your thighs, as you lay there, virgin territory to me, for all new lovers are virgins.

My tongue and lips moved ahead, searching out the sweet tender folds of flesh ...

Shit, thought Jay. Vulva. Sounds like a sink-plunger. Words, bloody words.

Your thighs are warm rain on my ears. I become a creature of water, my bones are liquid. My lips and tongue work around the hot smooth enfolding flesh, a sheer sweep from the hidden waking bud of ecstasy.

Clitoris: sounds like a precious literary magazine.

My finger slides inside you so easy, your body stretches and I hear you moan, or is it me? Another finger, you moan more and grab my hair by the roots, another finger, and you are seal-lovely, tugging and sinuous. Sally, you're fabulous. I want to have my whole hand inside you, roll in after, engulfed by you, and dance a flamenco inside you.

Vagina: Cleans Round The Bend. I am clean round the bend, thought Jay, opening her eyes and gulping crisp, white wine.

Inside you the muscles spring like steel and wrench at my knuckles as the blind fingers go deeper to the next gate of the golden land.

They call it a cervix. Sounds like a washing machine — the kind they show in adverts perched in the palm of a muscle-bound genie with a Superman kiss-curl.

It is the most intimate mouth, a sea-anemone caught unawares and as thrilling, flowing tentacles spring to my fingertips, Sally, you are beautiful, dragging deep breaths that shudder through your body, my body. The soles of your feet are on my back, kneading the pliant bones of my spine like a warm wave.

I want to please you. Lie number two: I want to drive you out of your mind. Lie number one was I want to sleep with you — I wanted to rip your clothes off and make love with you. Make love? Terribly prim for this desire to call it that.

My tongue laps at you, hair fills my mouth, my hand smoothes it away, and my tongue pirouettes against you. You grip my hand, your other arm flung over your head. Inside you my hand is caught like an ebb-tide sucks the sand from under your feet. My hand has become one with you and my face is melting into your cunt. Drink you, suck you, taste you, ripple into your blood and bones.

Your body stiffens, then trembles like an earthquake, you moan like you were giving birth. I want you to come, you want to come, and this isn't always easy with us barely being acquainted and all. But Sally, you're going to come if I stay here all night, because I am rooted between your thighs, growing inside your cunt, I am part of you and moaning as you moan, breathing this flow of joy like ozone ....

You make a sound like ripping a cork from the bottle with your teeth. From the base of my spine comes a hot jolt of elation and my mouth engulfs the open, pulsing bud of flesh and bone. It's so right. I will swallow you, grip you with my lips and drive my tongue into the tiny, elusive centre, my hand making catherine wheels inside you, and then you come. Spasms rip at me, your fabulous belly lashes like the core of a volcano, and I scramble to be on top of your body, your thighs holding me, the liquid fountains of joy thrumming me head to foot.

You nestle close, you might be crying, cry if you want to, Sally. Your head is on my shoulder and I kiss you with the tenderness I feel. You are so lovely. Close now. Be close now.

And then you laugh and smile with that mega-fab mouth of yours. You look me in the eye and say:

'That was a nice fuck. And a nice suck.'

It was, too.

You throw your head back on my arm and laugh with pleasure.

'And now let's have a drink. And share this awful cigarette I've rolled. I'll make a cup of tea and then, my dear,' you say, looking wicked, 'we'll get into your cunt.'

Goddammit, thought Jay, sparkling with delight. Fuck. Suck. Cunt. I like what your mouth does with these words.

I light a cigarette. Pee.

You are naked in your kitchen in the dark. I hold you, slide my hands round your beautiful breasts, your gorgeous arse, then slide my hands through your sodden hair, you are so wet and open. My hand dives inside you like a seal through waves, you cling and fall against me, I can hardly stand.

Later, on your bed, you say slowly and happily, 'I love being fucked.'

We are lying at an angle where I can give random kisses to your frankly astonishing body and each time I do, you stop what you're saying and draw a breath and shudder. I love your flesh. Am moved to your breast, take your nipple in my mouth and suck. Suck and fuck.

'Harder!' you say, and I swallow your breast, feels like a pomegranate, how easy it is to slip inside you. And how I love it, you love it.

I love your body rock 'n' rollin' along me, your lovely hands opening my cunt for your mouth to clamp onto, your tongue breaking me down to a fluid mass of sensation. Baby, baby, I swallow your fingers and feel the ripples up my spine. It's hard to come with a stranger, tense at taking so long, and to hell with it you are persistent, thoroughly fucking me. I come, black out for a second, two seconds, who knows? So uptight — you haven't noticed, and you rise up and say,

'What do you want? Tell me ...' so tender.

'Come up here and hold me,' I say and you hold me, I hold you too in a tight-fisted mine-all-mine of our flesh. You smooth my hair and say later,

'When you said, come here and hold me — were you just being polite?'

It's good to giggle. Could I be polite to you? The hell could I!

No, I say, no.

And, thought Jay, pulling on Wellingtons, hours and miles away from the city, tho' I had to go and didn't want to, I know we will maybe do do do do do it again and again ... and we will take more time. You kissed me goodbye, Sally in a long silky robe, so sweet, I don't want to go anywhere. Wanna wake up beside you and do do do do do-it-again.

We will if we want.

T'ain't nobody's bizness if we do.

Jay dreamed of filling her mouth with brandy and champagne and trickling into Sally's hot mouth.

It was not going to stop raining. She left the caravan and strode into the laughing teeth of a moorland wind. High on a tor, she turned, sudden tears in her eyes, sweeping the wild landscape and loving everything she saw.

THE FLAME

AMANDA HAYMAN

Cordelia peered into the mirror trying to decide if the whispy green tunic she was wearing was exactly the thing for tonight's ritual. Two serious brown eyes peered back, candlelight not being the best way of seeing oneself clearly. Cordelia was determined to set the mood early for the Big Night. She swayed a little from side-to-side, wondering if a spray of flowers in her hair would be over the top .....

Deena passed her forearm across her face, with the dual purpose of removing some of the sweat and pushing back her hair. It was too hot for ironing, but Rachel would barely have time to change when she got home from work. Deena had been back for two hours, during which time she'd managed to feed, bath and (she hoped) subdue three kids enough for the babysitter to cope. There, she'd finished Rachel's blue and white gingham — maybe she wouldn't bother with her own. But tonight was special — it'd be nice to make an effort.

At the thought of what was to come Deena felt a tug at her clit. Jeesus, it'd better be good. God knows (she mentally amended this to Goddess) it had been hard enough for her and Rachel waiting all this time .....

Sally set the empty champagne glass on the edge of the bath and stood up. Hmm, she'd need a shower — the only disadvantage of bubble bath was that it left her covered in bubbles. She ran the water first cold, then hot, then cold again. Her nipples responded to the change in temperature; her cunt nudged a response. Sally turned off the shower and surveyed her body. Thoughtfully, she ran the fingernails of her right hand lightly over her left nipple, and quickly withdrew them as sensation flooded over her. It wouldn't take much to reach the point of no return, and she must be strong for just a little longer .....

Amy was watching TV while she dried her long grey hair. On the table by the armchair was a mug of soup and a half-eaten piece of toast. Couldn't miss Coronation Street, not even for the Goddess herself. Good thing it was a warm night — the black vest and white shorts she was wearing would do fine. The ads started and Amy reached idly for her toast.

'Mummy, why is your head so soft?' droned the TV.

Amy stopped mid-chew as the scene changed and four women, arms crossed over naked breasts, jeans slung low on their hips, appeared. She was riveted by the softness of their skin and the suggestion of curves, and to her amazement she felt the unmistakable dampness of juices running in her crotch.

'For a heterocentric jeans ad?' she thought, 'Wow, am I ready for tonight ....'

Jan stood defiantly in the middle of the room, arms folded, eyes sparkling,

'What the fuck's wrong with you?' she screamed. 'You know I haven't had sex with anyone since the Equinox. It's got nothing to do with you.'

Melanie pouted and turned to look out the window. Jan strode across the room and grabbed the smaller woman's shoulders, forcing Melanie to look at her. They glared at each other fiercely for a minute, then Jan dropped her arms and sighed,

'You know I love you Mel, don't you?'

'Then why are you giving yourself to them tonight and not me?'

'Just one more day Mel. Tomorrow, anything you like.'

Melanie looked up with innocent eyes and grinned.

'It's only you who's got to wait isn't it?'

Jan nodded, wondering what was coming next. Slowly Melanie pushed her jeans down below her hips and kicked them away, displaying muscular legs and buttocks, and the triangle of light brown hair that Jan knew so well. Jan bit her lip and felt saliva fill her mouth as Melanie lay back on the bed and spread her legs, displaying her glories .....

Rachel stuffed her dirty overall into her bag and slung it over her shoulder. Wearily she wheeled her bike out of the car park as she contemplated the twenty-minute ride home. Really she was too tired to do anything except curl up on the sofa with a big, fat joint and vegetate. That Thursday night shift at Safeway was a killer — too bad the ritual had to be tonight. But solstices are no respecters of the schedules of mortals, and despite herself, Rachel felt a twinge of anticipation, radiating, she noticed with surprise, from between her legs. Oh well, maybe there was life left in the old dog yet .....

The six women stood in a circle in Amy's well-worn living room, now transformed by the thirteen silver candles that illuminated it and the heady smell of incense. They regarded each other gravely, with small uneasy smiles. Although they'd got to know each other pretty well over the thirteen weeks they'd been meeting, this was It. Could they do it, and would anything happen?

Amy took Sally and Jan's hands and gave them a reassuring squeeze. Without a word the others joined up, relaxing into the familiar pattern. Amy smiled up into Deena's watchful black eyes.

'Will you call the directions, Deena,' she said softly.

Sally and Cordelia let go of Deena and she stepped back from the circle, moving cat-like around it as she made offerings to the spirits of East, South, West and North, calling on them for their protection.

As she returned once more, her presence forming the link that closed the circle, each woman felt a whisper of energy pass into her, causing the expectation to mount. For a moment there was silence, and then Jan raised her head and looked around the circle, focussing on each woman in turn, until they returned the attention. She breathed deeply, from down in her belly, and one by one the others synchronized their rhythms. Cordelia had a sense of great peace and belonging, as though these other five beings were an integral part of herself.

Jan thought back to earlier in the evening, remembering how near she had been to excluding herself from this rite. Pleasuring Melanie, seeing her excitement grow and then climax in a great heave of relief, as the juices flowed from her cunt. It had been hard for Jan to stem her own desire. She swallowed, and licked lips, dry with tension, as some of those sensations returned at the thought.

'May we know the path by which we each stand here tonight?' she requested, looking from woman to woman and wondering if it had been easy for them. A murmur of assent went round, and Sally spoke.

'I guess I'm kind of surprised to be here tonight,' she began with a little laugh, 'When we wove our spell at Spring Equinox I barely believed I would be strong enough to go without sex, especially with myself.' She looked up shyly, but seeing no looks of disdain went on. 'You see right now, or at least until thirteen weeks ago, I was my own favorite lover.'

As she said this Sally ran her hands over the soft mounds of her enormous breasts, then lowered them to caress the multiple folds and swellings of her belly and thighs.

'Sometimes I didn't think I could resist sinking my fingers

into the wet, but I knew if I did I'd never stop, and I want to know what this could be like.'

She ceased abruptly as her cunt reminded her, in no uncertain terms, of just how long she'd been without.

Cordelia spoke next. 'You know, I never thought of myself as a sexual being,' she said dreamily, gazing at one of the candles that formed the perimeter of their circle. 'But somehow, knowing that I'd made a decision not to, I saw sex everywhere, even in my dreams. I kept thinking, "Supposing I come in the night, does that count?", but I never did, I'd get really turned on, and then wake up just before I could come. And my heart was beating wildly, and I'd just lie there on my back, rigid, waiting to calm down so I could go back to sleep. Somehow I think there may be more sex in my life after this.'

She smiled again, and nodded a little, lost in her own private reverie.

'Yeah, it was fucking difficult for me too,' said Jan, her voice edged with a faint note of bitterness. 'Mel figured out that just 'cos I couldn't come it meant she couldn't. And how could I deny her? Right before I came here this evening I had my head between her legs. And every time I licked her, my cunt screamed. Just one touch and I would've melted away, but like Sally, I'm curious.'

She tucked her thick blonde hair behind her ears and Deena saw the beads of sweat on her forehead glisten in the candlelight.

Rachel and Deena looked at each other across the circle. It was hard not to talk as a couple, especially in a situation like this, and if you hadn't told your lover everything you'd thought, well ....

'Well, my fantasies have gone bananas,' Rachel admitted and then continued quickly, 'We don't have sex that much after seven years, so I didn't think it would be too difficult, but I was wrong. Everytime I had a spare minute I found myself fantasizing about sex. Women I knew, women I didn't know, you name 'em, I had 'em, from Martina to Deena's sister.' A ripple went around the room, but Rachel didn't stop.

'And always the same thing. She'd get me stoned on some very exotic grass, grown especially to turn women on, and then she'd start to finger my nipples. My most sensitive part, you know,' said Rachel, with a half smile at Deena.

'She'd squeeze and pull and scratch and I'd writhe and pull her hand down to my throbbing cunt, but she wouldn't touch me or let me touch myself. I'd be really stoned, and all these incredible sensations would travel from my nipples to my cunt and back again. And she'd stop, and I'd do the same to her and we'd go on until we couldn't take any more.'

'I'm ready now.' Amy's voice, harsh with desire, cut across Rachel, who was now feeling her own nipples.

'Me too,' agreed Deena — for the last few minutes she had been massaging the muscular area of her belly just above her coarse, black pubic hair.

Sally reached to Amy on her left and Deena on her right, and gently began stroking their necks. Amy gasped and reached out her hand to Jan, who, having found her legs suddenly unsteady, was by now sitting against a large cushion. Remembering the words of not ten minutes before, and the bitterness of tone, Sally touched Jan lightly between the legs. The fierce heat burning through the thin fabric was not a surprise to her, and she moved her hand deeper. Jan groaned and put her hand on top of Sally's, trying to exert more pressure on her aching cunt.

Meanwhile Deena was exploring the pearly abundance that was Sally, taking great handfuls of breast and burying her face between them. Her fingers teased the area around the nipples. She heard Sally's breathing get shallower and realised she was not the only one paying homage to this treasure, as Amy was stroking

Sally's back and buttocks. Still teasing the large pink nipples, which by this time were as hard as gems, Deena moved behind Sally. This gave Amy the opportunity she was waiting for and she lay her head on the cushion of Sally's thigh and gently parted the sparse, brown hair. Sally caught her breath as Amy's tongue probed between her lips, which were being held open to display the swollen clitoris. Sally's hand continued to massage between Jan's legs. By this time Jan had removed all her clothes.

'Yes!' she screamed, alternating between kissing Cordelia, whose tongue seemed to know every pattern Sally was tracing in her cunt, and urging Sally to fuck her harder.

'Yes, oh please, don't stop!'

She felt Rachel's hand stroking, licking like fire, like ice everywhere on her body.

'Yeah, Jan honey, that's right. You're gonna come, just let us know how it feels ...' Rachel crooned.

For a second Cordelia glanced out of the circle, saw the candle flames join, dancing, leaping and surrounding them. A tongue of flame seemed to creep towards Jan and swirl around her.

Cordelia was jolted back into the rite by the feeling of her nipples being caressed by Jan who was moaning in abandon; Sally's fingers were crawling inside her growing vagina as the thumb rubbed up and down, over the very head of her clitoris. Jan came, bucking and squeezing her legs. She screamed wildly as her orgasm exploded.

Amy saw that flame too, she saw a thin wisp coil from Jan, to encircle Sally whose hand was now beside Amy's tongue, toying with her own labia. Sally climaxed strongly, knowing she would, knowing she could wait for the tongue that travelled lazily from the beginning of her cunt to high inside her vagina. The spasms were powerful and she shouted with each. Never had it gone on so long before, that deep, satisfying throb of cunt that rhythmically repeated. It went on, even though Amy had moved her face and was now kissing Sally's belly. Sally grasped Jan's hand.

'You too?' she whispered.

Jan nodded and continued with her venture of making Rachel's fantasy come true. From the tone of the groans that accompanied this, there was no doubt she was succeeding.

Amy lay on her back and reached up a hand to stroke Deena's gleaming body. Deena held Amy's gaze for a second, then lowered herself on top of her. Savagely, Deena's hand worked Amy's crotch, forcing the seam of her shorts into the folds of her delicate flesh. To Amy, the friction was delicious and she squirmed to make the connection tighter. Great waves of exquisite sensations ran over her, until she felt there was nothing in the world but her cunt and Deena's hand. Just when she knew she must come, the pressure suddenly stopped and she felt her shorts being dragged off. The rubbing started up again, but this time it was a hundred times sharper, clearer, brighter. Fingers probed the sensitive crevices along the sides of her clit, at the entrance of her vagina.

'Ohh, ohhh,' she sobbed, 'Oh now! Now!'

The fingers flicked her clit gently and went away. Amy nearly screamed with frustration, but then the exploration continued. Fingering her hair, pulling gently; opening out her lips so she was exposed, waiting for the touch. And it came, came, came. At that point, Amy knew she was part of the flame. She looked up again at Deena, crouching over her. She was panting too. Gently Amy drew Deena down until she could reach that delectable cunt with her tongue. Deena straddled Amy's face, opened herself to the eager seeking. Long firm strokes with no respite. Deena's cunt purred and she moaned with the pleasure of having her clit sucked so avidly.

Women's bodies, decided Cordelia, are all beautiful and all different. She was making loose, flowing patterns on Rachel's sweating skin. Between the ministrations of Jan and Cordelia, it seemed likely that Rachel would come any minute. Cordelia herself was pretty turned on too, and this time, thank the goddess, it wasn't a dream. Not with the heat building like this, her very centre turning to molten silver. Wait a minute, it's Rachel being touched, not me, but I'm coming too.

'Oh, wow! Oh, yeesss!'

And Cordelia knew it was the flame itself that had caressed her, given her this joy as the circle was once more completed.

Together they lay on the floor and the cushions, their bodies drained by a surfeit of sensuality. Yet they did not sleep, for each of them in her own thoughts knew she had done 'it' and that sex magic had been with them this night, and that it was the most sacred magic of all.

The circle is ever open, never unbroken
The Goddess be with you wherever you are,
Merry meet and merry part, and merry meet again.

LIVING AS A LESBIAN RAMBLING

CHERYL CLARKE

Cleo wants to break up with Doris. She confides to me:

'Truth be told sharing a bed with one body
gets into places the fucking don't. It makes
for need where there wasn't none. The sleeping
together does. If I leave Doris, I'll have to
find somebody else to sleep with. That's the
drag of it all. The leaving that is.'

Doris writes Cleo a post card from across the street:

'When I can't suck your pussy,
I put sugar, cigarettes, marijuana,
caffeine, and alfalfa sprouts in my mouth.'

And here I am, here having been left.
My body wants hers so bad I am almost relieved
she said no. And then goodbye.
The last Wallenda on the high wire
that day the wind changed.
Witholding and demanding,
I never said, 'love' unless you said it first
and you never said 'make love' unless
I said it first.
Still I travelled with trucks, tractors, trailers,
flat beds, campers, cabs, wide and oversize loads
to sleep with you. Whales logging against medians.

Swimmers of the great macadams. I sailed their
back winds, swerved to avoid their fish tails, jack
knifes, and blown-off treads, crashed their caravans,
inhaled their fumes, to go to bed with you.

Our reunion was intended for this century.
I know her from before. In the dream it is a
desert of some other dusty, desolate place like
southeast DC. People walk and carry their
houses on their backs. From North Carolina to
Oklahoma, I want to know the Trail of Tears only
to return to search the Great Smokeys for those of
my people who refused to leave.

I've gotten you confused with that runaway
sister I shared a bed with, who left me
and my faithful half-brother to our incorrigible
mother — grief so unrelenting she could not
console us. My brother ran away to the army
soon after. Too late for Korea he deserted
and disappeared, his passion to draw numbed
by whisky, fighting, and hatred of white men.

I'm travellin light.* My clothes could fit a
matchbox.** I use a camera for passion.
Away from the cities that knew us in this life.
I cultivated the barrell cactus, prickly heart on
green sleeve. Make pets of armadillos. Carry
no medicine for snake bites. And hallucinate
'til you find me and make your pallet beside mine
in the land-locked places our great-grandmothers
knew. In the 117 degree sun I am lonely and regret
the times I was too defiant to come.

Outside a laundromat in chemical Elizabeth
I follow a man, rouged like my mother,

billowing yellow dress over dark camisole
over rhythms measured and random hips like my
mother, forgetting, I call 'Mama' to him, boldly,
sweetly he accepts my sadness, takes my arm,
makes me sit with him pulls his hem to his
crotch spreads his ample thighs and to my
chapped lips kisses his palm full with the
scent of yerba buena.

Pumpkins punctuate green hills.
Off on a cliff above the ocean a lone
palm tree sweeps the wind, leaves akimbo
and then redwoods, tall as mountains. And
she sends me a dozen yellow roses in Berkeley.
The card says:
   'And we can still be friends.'
Each day I wear one in my buttonhole or behind
my ear. I wear the last one pinned to my green
lapel. She nearly withers during the delay in
Baltimore. I revive her in Newark. She spreads
herself finally in a short glass of water with a
wide mouth. I send her two pairs of my dirty
bikini briefs and a scribbled poem in plain
brown wrapper:
   'And that's how it is.
   Truth be told.
   I can't be without somebody to sleep with.
   It's the body.
   A woman's — must be a woman's.
   And yours was superb and particular
   for arms, legs, breasts
   supplanting the seduction of dreams.'

* 'I'm Travelin' Light,' as sung by Billie Holiday.
** 'Billie's Blues,' written and sung by Billie Holiday.

NIGHT SMELLS

RUTH BOWEN

Garlic: fried with almonds and courgettes
            lingers on the stairs
            as I dash shivering to the loo

Toothpaste: chemical mint and fluoride
            oozes from the uncapped tube
            as I turn to rinse my hands

Freesias: bought in shy celebration of your visit
            fill my room

Rosewater: distilled in creams designed to iron out age
            mingles with your final cigarette
            as I lean to kiss
            now sleeping lips

Woman: adjusting the pillow
            I catch an unexpected echo of your hot wetness
            left on fingers that had earlier
            reached you

WATER WITH THE WINE

JEWELLE GOMEZ

Alberta applied the fresh red to her lips under the glare of the bathroom fluorescents and smoothed the soft folds of her tan, linen skirt. She sighed, then drew a deep breath, gathering her energy for the final event, a small reception for out-of-town speakers given by a local women's writing group. The conference had gone well. Alberta was pleased with her presentation on sexuality in women's literature, although at first she'd been leery of being the only black writer and the only out lesbian on the conference programme.

The participants were attentive and even excited about a new perspective. Tomorrow she'd board a plane for one more speaking engagement before hurrying back to Boston to collapse for two days then prepare for fall classes in the remaining weeks of summer.

She let herself relax for a moment as she walked back down the corridor to the college's small reception room then set herself for the light banter and the rather personal questions people put to visiting writers. When she turned to the table to refill her glass with white wine she reached for the carafe at the same time as a young woman, whose face she recognized from the question and answer period during her presentation. She was a short, blond woman who looked like an athlete. Tonight she looked rather different in the soft leather trousers and silk shirt but Alberta could not forget the brilliant smile and sharp eyes as the woman laughed at their collision. She introduced herself as Emma and they sat on one of the couches against the wall away from the swirl of writers and students. Alberta remembered with pleasure the way Emma had participated in the discussion which followed her presentation, not just drawing out information but projecting her own ideas into the discourse.

'I really appreciated your frankness when you were asked about sadomasochism and the lesbian movement,' Emma said.

Alberta laughed. It always took her aback to have the term just blurted out by students in this type of surrounding even when she herself had used it so casually in the lecture hall. She guessed that was simply a function of her age. Even with progressive ideas, at forty, Alberta felt a bit demure sometimes.

'Well,' she started, 'unlike some feminists, I don't think there are some things that should not be discussed. The Victorian attitude is not a luxury we can afford. In fact if it's difficult to discuss all the more reason to bring it up.'

Alberta's eyes caught the silver labyris which hung against Emma's freckled chest and said,

'Living out here I'm sure you can understand that.'

'Of course, in the abstract or on a one-to-one basis, but being put on the spot like that ... you were the only black writer and then the only one doing a presentation on sexuality, I don't know what I'd do, especially when asked to represent an entire school of thought, so to speak.'

They both laughed and Alberta looked more directly at the woman who was about twenty-five and had a wonderfully impish smile.

'Girl, it looks like somebody's always going to be asked to represent something. We might as well prepare ourselves.' Alberta was not certain why fifteen years could feel so large a span of time in some circumstances and so small in others. Right now she felt closer to this woman than to anyone in the room, including her ex-lover, the English professor who'd invited her to Missouri to participate in the conference and had been studiously avoiding her ever since.

By the time Alberta finished the thought in her head Emma was back to the panel discussion asking questions about Hurston and Lorde, not using the hushed tones that nascent writers sink to but driving her questions with ebulliant enthusiasm, as if she knew these writers intimately.

'But if, as you said, the impulse to dramatic sexual expression, as you called it, is present in all of us, why don't you see it more in young black writers; why is it so awkwardly prevalent in the writing of white women?'

'Socialization, sublimation, any number of reasons. Not seeing it explicitly in someone's writing or conversation doesn't mean it doesn't exist. Some people are more private than others, even within themselves.'

Alberta caught Liza's glance for a moment just then and thought how true that was. Professor Liza, so private even she didn't know her own feelings. Her move to Missouri had not been discussed. Alberta was told one evening Liza was going to take the post and Alberta would be left behind. That had been over a year ago and still Liza didn't acknowledge how angry Alberta had been at her. This invitation seemed like an attempt to pretend there was no reason for anger. By now Alberta ignored the subtext and simply accepted the check and added the college's name to her résumé. If Liza wanted to avoid unpleasantness by substituting a formal professional relationship for an honest friendship, fine. Alberta could bear a chill with the best of them. She ignored her friends who said bitterly, 'That's a white woman for you!' and thought simply 'That's Professor Liza Harris for you' and turned back to the young woman, Emma, whose enthusiasm was so infectious.

Conversation swelled around them and they had to lean a little closer to be heard. Alberta found herself trying not to gaze at the soft swell of Emma's breasts beneath the red silk as they rose and fell with her excitement.

'Listen, I really want to talk more but this crowd is driving me mad,' Emma said, 'Would you like to go for coffee or something else to wash out the taste of collegiate wine?'

Alberta glanced at her watch. It was still early but she'd done her duty here. Her plane wasn't until 1 pm the next afternoon. She nodded gratefully and they stood and moved toward the door. Liza reached them just as Alberta turned back remembering she should say goodbye to someone.

'Berta, just let me know when you're ready, I'll get you back to your hotel,' Liza said with a bit of stiff curiosity.

'No need, sweetheart,' Alberta said with an engaging smile, enjoying this bit of dancing, 'I've got a ride right here. This was a great event. You should be proud. I'll call you when I finally get back to Beantown.'

She planted a quick kiss on the silver hair at Liza's temple and exited quickly. Emma was already halfway down the hall. In five minutes they were seated in Emma's battered Chevrolet. Twenty minutes later she was not surprised when they pulled up in front of a small, woodframe house on a shaded street.

'We might as well have it here. I don't think anything's left open in this town at this hour. Except maybe the leather bars.' Emma said this with that same impish look and they both laughed loudly in the quiet darkness as they entered the house.

'I thought my roommate might be home but looks like she's out.'

Seated on the couch they sipped white wine spritzers enjoying their coolness in the still, hot evening. They talked about

Emma's graduate work in American literature under the quiet hum of an old fan and a Joan Armatrading tape Emma had clicked on almost unconsciously as soon as she'd cleared a space on the couch. Books lined the walls and stacks of papers strewn across a desk at the other end of the room identified it as the home of a scholar.

'I think you must need some theatrical training to do this kind of thing, going around to campuses answering personal questions. You just drew a breath and sounded like discussing nipple piercing was the most natural thing in the world.'

'Believe me, it's not casual. I used to be so nervous my voice quavered. I see those faces out there trying to suppress their disapproval until they can find a discretely academic way to put me down, either because I'm a lesbian or because I seem to be advocating something they perceive as violence against women. But then I see those other faces. Like yours. Those that aren't afraid of knowledge.'

'Are you? Advocating, I mean.'

'I don't have to advocate. People find their own expressions of desire whatever the moral majority or the politically correct condemn. Lesbians should be the first to know that. And if I wanted to stop whatever the majority disapproved of I'd have to start by figuring out how not to be black.'

As they laughed again, Alberta kicked off her shoes and before she knew it Emma was on the carpet massaging her feet. She didn't think to protest. It felt good. She rested her head on the back of the worn sofa and let her mind wander. Liza appeared briefly in her thoughts but then she saw Emma's smile and smiled herself.

'Ticklish?'

'No, just thinking.'

'What?' Emma asked.

'Um ... What Liza, Professor Harris would say if she could see us now. She's one of those sticklers for correctness. I think this might appear to be an act of exploitation!'

'Or an act of seduction,' Emma responded.

'Who's seducing whom?' Alberta said trying to keep her voice steady, feeling Emma's strong hand on her calf.

Emma kneeled on the edge of the sofa, towering over Alberta's face, 'I'll seduce first then you can seduce next, just to keep it egalitarian.' She leaned down and stopped any response with her mouth. She pressed downward and let her hand brush Alberta's short Afro haircut softly.

Alberta was startled and for a moment uncertain how she wanted to respond. She was used to come-ons from students. And had even been in tight spots that required embarrassing firmness. But she'd not been here before. She wanted this kiss. She'd known it as soon as she felt Emma's hand on her. But she felt torn between so many things. Liza's horror, which she knew lurked somewhere in the distance, her own sense of propriety that had often helped her through tough emotional situations but now clung to her with all the comfort of one of those panty-girdles she'd given up so long ago.

Emma held her mouth pressed to Alberta's until she felt a response. She then pulled back and said, 'I've wanted to do that since the panel discussion. It was all I could do to figure out how to be alone with you. I considered following you to the ladies room when you slipped out but I opted for something a little more elegant.'

Again their laughter filled the room and Alberta knew it was a sound she wanted to hear again and again. She brushed Emma's hair back from her forehead and pulled her mouth back down to her own. She caught her breath with the excitement. The scent of Emma's sweat and the leather filled her head. Emma straddled her lap pinning her against the back of the couch in a supple movement that didn't even break their kiss. Alberta strained upward against Emma's weight, reaching out for the heat she felt.

'Lift.' Emma said raising herself a little from Alberta. When Alberta was able to raise herself a bit on the creaking sofa, Emma reached down and slid the linen skirt up Alberta's thighs. It slid softly on the nylon slip and stockings up around her waist. Alberta caught herself worrying about the wrinkles. She had planned to wear the suit at her next engagement.

'There's always room service,' Emma said, as if reading her mind. Again the laughter surrounded them making a bond that little explicit knowledge could create so quickly.

Alberta's laughter turned to a gasp as she felt Emma's hand plunge inside of her stockings, then inside of her.

Emma sucked in her breath kissing her deeply. Her tongue touched her teeth then sought out Alberta's tongue while her hand pushed inside her for her wetness. Alberta pressed forward loving the touch of Emma's mouth and tongue. She drew back only to catch her breath but Emma pursued her mouth grasping her head with one hand. Her other pushed deeper inside Alberta's cunt.

'Oh, god! Alberta.' She said not believing the joy she felt at touching this woman. Her hand moved gently for a moment. She kissed the side of Alberta's face, her hair, her ear, finally resting her forehead on the sofa beside Alberta as all of her energy went through her hand into Alberta's body. She pushed hard, the full force of her body inside of Alberta. The wetness deluged her fingers as she worked deeper. She felt only the desire like a tide wiping out all thought of anything else. She wanted Alberta as she'd never wanted anyone before. 'Please, baby,' she moaned in Alberta's ear, thrusting inside of her, almost swooning herself at the feel of Alberta straining upward to take in more of her. Alberta's voice was hoarse with desire as she tried to hold in her screams,

'Yes, yes,' she said over and over again as she came.

They sat sprawled silently for many minutes until they both caught their breath. Emma climbed over Alberta, remaining on her knees looking into Alberta's eyes. She took in the sweet darkness of Alberta's skin and eyes. Her own pale brown eyes were pin points of desire. The tape ended. Joan Armatrading's deep voice no longer masked their uneven breathing.

'Come,' Emma said standing in front of the couch, 'we'll go back to your hotel. You can leave your suit to be pressed. I'll take you to the airport tomorrow.'

'You really do think fast, don't you?'

'I had to have some kind of plan just in case you said yes. And you really did say yes, didn't you.' Emma said, as she pulled Alberta to her feet. Without her heels she was not quite that much taller than Emma. She wrapped her arms around Alberta kissing her with a feeling that let Alberta know this was still only the beginning of the evening. Less than an hour later they were curled around each other's bodies in the Holiday Inn.

The next day, on the plane Alberta stared at the piece of notebook paper Emma had given her with her address and phone number, as if to assure herself she'd not dreamed the entire event. But it had not been a dream. Emma had been there in the morning when Liza called asking to take her to breakfast. They'd almost had one of their circuitous fights as Alberta tried to decline the invitation graciously and Emma discreetly showered. At the airport they both remembered they didn't know each other very well and tried not to feel conspicuous although they felt everyone could look at them and tell how they'd spent their night. Alberta wasn't certain whether she felt uncomfortable with the formality of giving Emma her card as they separated, or if she simply felt uncomfortable giving anything at all. A non-commital goodbye would have been better she thought, but wasn't certain so turned her mind to her next engagement. She would have a full day on campus to re-orient herself and go over notes before her lecture on women in the Harlem Renaissance. She tried to push Emma into the back of her mind. But when she closed her eyes she could still feel her hand inside of her. The feeling stayed with Alberta throughout the rest of her trip, it remained with her back home in Boston and into the fall.

◆ ◆ ◆

Settled comfortably in the small booth of Bob the Chef's Restaurant Alberta shoved her Christmas shopping bags under the table between her legs. Marsh did the same across from her, sweat gleaming on her caramel coloured forehead. Her tightly pressed hair was pulled back in a bun, glistening under the bright lights of the old and familiar spot.

'I'm tell you girl. I look at your figures and they just don't add up worth shit!'

Alberta always marvelled at how quickly Marsha dropped the clipped tones she used at work in the insurance company and reverted to their southern-tinged vernacular when they discussed their personal lives.

'I don't know what I'd do with her, here I mean.'

'Don't they have a saying out there, "I'm from Missouri, Show Me". Seems like the girl done told you what to do with her. Here or anywhere!' Marsha said with the same mischievous sparkle Alberta had enjoyed since they were in high school together. She didn't remember now why she and Marsh weren't still lovers but that had been a while ago and having her as a friend was one of the most important events in her life.

'She's twenty-five years old, Marsha!'

'She ain't askin' you to adopt her!'

'She's, well, she's not black.'

'I can only repeat myself.'

They were silent as the waitress came and took their order.

'From what I gather she's only five foot five too. Maybe you better not have dinner with her.'

They both smiled at that while Alberta tried to re-phrase her objections.

'I just can't figure you either, Marsha. Why are you so hot on this? You never liked Liza.'

'Listen, anybody who dares to be a dyke and wear black leather pants in a Missouri college, anybody who sends you Alison Bechdel cartoon post cards, anyone who can seduce you in the same state in which Liza Harris lurks, I like!'

Whenever Alberta wondered why she'd remained in Boston she thought of Marsha. Although she'd often felt alone after her mother died, leaving only a distant cousin she'd only recently come to know, she thought of Marsha as her family.

'It's taken you a year to get away from the memories of Liza. Don't fall back on all those excuses. Either you like the girl or you don't. And since you keep those postcards up in your office it looks like 'like' to me.'

'Well maybe we can have drinks. She may not have much time. She said she's going to be visiting some friends in Cambridge so she might not have a lot of time.'

'Listen do you want to do something together. Maybe we could have dinner together or something.'

'I don't know, Marsha. I have to wait and see.'

'Okay, fine but take a look and see, okay?'

Alberta was silent.

'Berta?'

'Okay, it can't hurt. She is really nice and ...'

'Please don't start on that part, I can't bare to discuss sex when I'm eating chicken and dumplings.'

◆ ◆ ◆

The conversation with Marsha replayed itself in Alberta's head as she waited in front of the 'T' station on Massachusetts Avenue near Commonwealth Avenue. She wondered how she looked in her tan wool slacks and matching sweater. She'd given herself a haircut and was checking herself in her rearview mirror when she felt Emma's presence beside the car. Her heart leapt in her chest but she leaned over casually to unlock the door. When Emma slid into the passenger's seat, the car lit up with her smile. Alberta gazed at those pale eyes and the way her hair flew away from her face and couldn't remember why she'd been so afraid. Emma cupped Alberta's face in her hands and placed a tender kiss on her mouth that left Alberta trembling.

'I'm so happy to see you at last. I can't tell you how happy. Only show you.' Emma said.

Alberta laughed nervously. She felt suddenly shy.

'I guess, lunch can wait a while.'

'No, lunch can't wait at all. Where do you live?' Emma answered, lowering her voice as she leaned into Alberta's ear to plant a small kiss on her neck.

Alberta made a U-turn on Massachusetts Avenue and drove smoothly back to the South End. She felt proud showing Emma her house, one she'd lived in since graduate school. She'd been able to buy it before the wave of upwardly mobile, and mostly white, professionals had discovered the crumbling South End and decided to make it theirs. She was one of the few in her neighborhood who remembered its history. She remembered the Hi Hat bar where her mother had been a bar maid. Billie Holiday had made that one of her hangouts in her hey day. And Charlie's Sandwich Shop which now catered to investment bankers used to be the one neutral territory for the ladies of the evening who used to work Columbus Avenue. They could slip in for breakfast and not be harassed by johns, pimps or policemen.

She didn't tell Emma any of this as she showed her the house. As she poured some juice for both of them Emma asked,

'Is this where you and Liza Harris lived?'

'Shit!' Alberta said before she knew it. Then recovering herself she said evenly, 'She never lived here. She had a place in the Back Bay. I guess college town talk is the same whether it's in Massachusetts or Missouri.'

'There wasn't any talk really. I knew that Prof. Harris had come out from teaching at Boston University. And then the attitude she gave us as we were leaving, then the morning phone call sort of made me think about it. When she dropped by the teaching assistant's office one evening, and so carefully and casually asked me to stop for a drink with her, I knew she wanted to know what had gone between you and I, and it wasn't purely professional. She's a bit of a bitch, I'd say.'

'That's bit of an understatement!'

Emma was as relieved to hear those words as Alberta was to finally say them. During the entire flight to Boston she'd meticulously reviewed what little she knew just as she'd done all fall. She wondered if they were still involved, if that was why Alberta had never contacted her. When she'd checked into the hotel she felt foolish, having devised this scheme, faking a visit to non-existent friends in Cambridge simply to have an excuse to offer a casual meeting. If Alberta had not responded she'd been determined to come anyway. Her next move had remained a mystery but now it was clear. She would have found Alberta. Their meeting would not have been as casual. This was what she wanted and short of Alberta telling her to her face 'Get out of my life!', Emma had no intention of leaving the empty space between them. Emma drew Alberta into her arms not yet ready to tell Alberta all of this but hoping to show her.

After they'd sipped their juice for a moment Emma said,

'I want to make love to you. I want you now.'

They walked silently upstairs to the bedroom which was bathed in bright afternoon light. They both watched each other as they removed their clothes. Alberta draped hers, carefully, over an armchair that was covered in richly coloured African-print material. Emma stepped out of her jeans and tossed her bright blue, wool shirt onto the chair atop Alberta's tan outfit. When Alberta bent over the bed to pull back the comforter, Emma leaned against her back and pressed her down onto the bed. She rubbed her hand across the broadness of Alberta's back, enjoying the feel of her skin and the pale colour of her hand against the darkness of Alberta's flesh. The one other time she'd slept with a black woman the combination of colours had not struck her so strongly. Now she could barely breathe just watching the contrast and feeling the suppleness of Alberta's body as it began to respond to the pressure of her own.

She kissed the back of Alberta's neck then slid down to kiss her back in repeated rows back and forth until she'd covered all of her skin. She could see Alberta's breath beginning to come faster as she lowered herself again atop her. She slid one hand down to spread Alberta's legs further apart. Then rubbed the inside of her thighs methodically.

'You know I feel like I should go slowly. I want to go slowly. That will have to be later. I want you right now. You know that I can't wait.' With that, she pushed one finger inside of Alberta's cunt from behind. She moved slowly at first, then worked another finger inside while Alberta gasped for breath. She reached up and clutched Alberta's wrist against the pillow giving herself leverage as she pushed inside, harder. Fulfilling the dream she'd had since the last time they'd seen each other. Her fingers worked quickly then, determined to reach their desire, to feel the flood of Alberta's desire around them.

'Now, baby, now! Now!' Emma cried out and Alberta came for her more quickly than she'd ever come before.

Emma let her body relax against Alberta's back, but Alberta was not weakened by this explosion of energy. She rolled Emma from her and onto her back. She moved down to Emma's breast taking the small pink nipple into her mouth. Rolling her tongue over it, sucking it in as deeply as she could, then nipping it with her teeth until she heard Emma's sharp intake of breath and Alberta felt the quiver pass through her body. Then down to the pale blondish-coloured hair between Emma's thighs. She licked around the edges of Emma's cunt enjoying the musky smell and each gasp from Emma as she got close to the lip of her cunt. She glanced up at Emma's face. Her eyes opened and closed as if she could not believe the pleasure she felt. They opened wider than anything Alberta had ever seen. Then Alberta sunk her tongue inside of Emma and watched the rush of red to Emma's face as she moaned. Then Alberta realized that in all of her lovemaking, with Liza, with anyone, she'd never wanted to take a lover as much as she herself had wanted to be taken. Until now. Now she breathed only to hear Emma come. She flicked her tongue across the pointed hardness of Emma's clit. Then drew it inside her mouth as she'd done Emma's nipple, sucking it then pressing it between her teeth, gently, then harshly, until Emma's body convulsed with the coming orgasm.

Quickly Alberta slid her finger into Emma's wet cunt, underneath her tongue, pushing rhythmically, unceasingly, until Emma screamed wildly. After, her body shook with the final wave of orgasm Alberta pulled herself up so she lay fully atop Emma's body.

They fell into a light sleep as the sun moved, first slowly, then quickly across the sky, leaving a reddish light across the room then darkness.

They woke many times during the night to explore each other, then finally slept deeply when the darkest part of night quieted the room and the city outside.

In the morning Emma was still too uncertain of her position to reveal her deception. As Alberta prepared tea and mixed a batch of quick cornbread she asked that Alberta drop her back at the 'T' station so she could 'say goodbye to her friends' before she left for the airport.

As they sat enjoying the light breakfast, Emma felt full of words but was stifled by knowledge of the few hours that lay before them and anxiety about how much or how little Alberta wanted to share with her. Their intermittent discussion of books and writing had been full of enthusiasm and as much passion as their lovemaking, but beyond that lay a shadowy gulf which Emma was unsure how to bridge. She felt confounded by Alberta's casual pleasantness and as they began to leave, she felt her anger rise and knew she must speak before this visit ended.

'This has been one of the most important experiences of my life,' Emma said, fearing the ominous portent that seemed to hang in the air as soon as the words were out of her mouth. Still she continued,

'I have to say, though, that I feel a kind of disrespect from you. I'm not sure that's just the word I want to use. But it's what comes out. I can tell you want to be with me, but there's this side of you that doesn't take me seriously, or something. You think I'm smart, carry on a good conversation and I'm good in bed but then some kind of wall goes up as if you think I'm not worth the trouble of knowing. Maybe it means something else to you but I can't really tell from this side and it pisses me off.'

'Disrespect has nothing to do with it. You don't realize what I've made of myself, my life. You can't expect me to throw myself into something that doesn't even make sense to me. I don't know you.'

'Do you want to? That's the question I have. I get the feeling that if I hadn't had to be in town this weekend you never would have written or called me. Do you want to know me?'

'I don't know, Emma. Right now, I don't know.'

Somehow Emma felt relief at that admission, just as Alberta did at finally hearing Emma's questions. Before she opened the door she moved closer to Emma and reached out to stroke the soft blonde curls that framed her face. She pulled her to her and kissed her solidly on her mouth. They held each other for a few minutes then stepped out into the bright, late morning sun.

Back in Missouri, Emma embraced its icy-cold winter enthusiastically. She hiked, went skiing and worked on her thesis, happy to have the stringent weather and writing absorb most of her energy. She'd made job inquiries in California and Massachusetts although the University had invited her to stay on and teach, at least for one semester.

It was only when alone in her room late at night that the decisions about her future held no comfort. Laying in bed, making lists in her head of work for the next day, she imagined when she might venture another note to Alberta. She was thrilled to receive a chatty post card from her but still felt unsatisfied with Alberta's discreet message and obvious ambivalence. She tried to understand her cautiousness but was impatient with her inability to explore the relationship their desire was drawing them into.

She turned abruptly onto her side, trying to escape the image of Alberta's face which filled her head. She composed a long letter in her mind, describing to Alberta the enormity of what she felt. As she drifted into sleep she know it was not a letter she would write until Alberta showed she too was willing to open herself, a little. Winter sleep was best, there were fewer dreams.

◆ ◆ ◆

'Umm, Missouri seems to be slipping. This looks like the same post card on your bookcase since the last time I was here.' Marsha said, slyly turning one over to read the message.

'Stop being so nosey!'

Marsha finished reading then said, as she walked to the couch,

'That girl sure got a way with words, umph, umph, umph.' She sipped from the glass of wine Alberta placed on the table, not speaking for a while. She watched Alberta shifting in her seat for a moment then said,

'There ain't been this much dead air in here since what's her name left town. Maybe you better spit it out before it gets much later in the evening.'

'I hate when you do that Marsha. Her name is Liza ...'

'Okay, okay. Don't try to change my direction. What's on your mind or should I be asking what's up in Missouri?'

'I'm thinking of going out there to visit her.'

'Thinking?'

'Well I've got a reservation for a flight. I might or might not use it. I don't know yet.'

'Correct me if I'm wrong but didn't we have a similar conversation sometime this winter. Girl, it's spring, I can't spend my time repeating myself when I have to get my May wardrobe together.'

Alberta was silent. Sometimes Marsha's abrupt style and keen intuition made Alberta angry. She felt exposed and somewhat juvenile, agonizing over something Marsha had already so easily analysed and disposed of. Alberta shifted on the couch, ignoring Marsha's penetrating stare. Alberta raked her fingers through her short, dark Afro and stared at the digital lights on the stereo as if they were instruments for forecasting the future.

'Okay, let me cut to the chase for you. You made these reservations and you're afraid to go because she might reject you, or worse might be thrilled to see you and that would mean you have to respond in some responsible way, like admitting you adore her and want to make more of it. How am I doing so far?'

Alberta said nothing.

'Okay. So you've got to get out there and check her out before you go mad with desire and loneliness but you think whatever happens out there, back here, people will be waiting at the airport for your return to cast aspersions on you character and perhaps even stones on you body for pursuing a younger, whiter woman. And then there's what's her name, you 'ex', who will probably be lurking in the bush to be certain to witness whatever happens between you and Emma and be certain it makes the six o'clock news, preferably national. Then the bank will call in your mortgage on this house, you few remaining relatives, whom you speak to seldom will disinherit you. And the last but certainly not the least of the retributions: I, your oldest friend, will find you ridiculous and withdraw my friendship.'

Marsha stopped hoping to hear laughter from Alberta. Instead there was silence. When she looked closely she saw tears forming under Alberta's closed lashes.

'Oh baby, I'm sorry, I didn't mean to make you cry. But it's true the last one is the most terrible possibility. Except I got it all backwards. If you don't get on a plane and go see this woman I'm going to beat you senseless. I know all those other things are scary but you've got it bad and you can't be afraid of trying again no matter what the odds are. Come on, did we or did we not sit in at the Provost's office in 1969 until they took us to jail. Did we or did we not go after those guys in Dorchester with tire irons when they kept driving by my apartment yelling 'dyke.' When you told your mother you were in love with what's ... I mean with Liza, didn't your mother invite her to dinner two days after she swore she'd never let her set foot in her house?'

Marsha moved closer to Alberta and held her in her arms and listened to soft sobs.

'Come on we survived 50s television, you're not going to let being in love scare you into paralysis are you?'

Finally Marsha heard a soft giggle among the tears.

'I'll even take you to the airport just like I did the first time you went out of town for a speaking engagement. Remember how we got drunk in the airport bar at 10 am. Come on.'

'My flight's at noon two weeks from tomorrow. I haven't let Emma know I want to come out yet.'

'I'll take the day off in case I get a hangover.'

◆ ◆ ◆

Emma sat in the airport bar sipping her Rolling Rock. She arrived an hour early — completely at odds with her feelings. Part of her was so excited that Alberta was finally coming to see her she couldn't keep her hands from trembling, nor could she keep the moisture from seeping through her panties to her jeans. She'd changed shirts three times and looking now in the smoked mirror of the bar she felt totally over dressed for what was supposed to be a casual visit. The other part of Emma was angry at that: the casual visit. Alberta's phone call had been a wonderful surprise but Emma was not sure she wanted to be an amusing stopover as Alberta went on to another college, another conference and left her behind. Her own studies were going well; she had thrown herself into the work on her master's thesis, thinking that would get her through the winter and spring. Somehow, once free of that obligation, she'd be able to plan what to do next. How to approach a career, how to approach Alberta. But she was determined not to spend her summer inventing ways to see Alberta. All of the time pretending she didn't mind appearing to be a light entertainment in Alberta's life, which seemed, from this distance and with little or no communication, to be hung up on her past relationship with Liza Harris and securing her career in Boston.

Emma sat the bottle down with a thud. 'Forget that! What the hell am I? Some hick from the sticks? Midwest may not be New York but I got things to do too, shit!'

Emma glanced at her watch and realized she'd be late for the landing if she continued sitting talking to herself.

She spotted Alberta coming down the corridor easily. She was one of the few black faces in the line of rumple-suited businessmen. But apart from that, her bearing was distinctive. She moved from side-to-side. She carried a week-ender bag and her briefcase as if they had no weight at all, keeping her shoulders even and her head high. Emma forgot all of her resolves for the moment and ran forward to hold Alberta in her arms. She didn't care that the passengers surrounding them were gaping at her. Men were always made uneasy by women moving fast, and fearful of women showing love for each other. She threw herself into Alberta's arms as if she'd not noticed anyone in the entire airport. The ride home was quick and comfortable. Questions and answers about her thesis filled their conversation until they sat at the kitchen table and Emma served Alberta the glass of juice which she requested to wash down a couple of aspirins.

'It's just a little headache, it will be gone in a while.'

Emma sat anxiously watching Alberta's face. Looking for signs of something but decided to wait before taking up any serious conversation.

'My best friend, Marsha and I have a little ritual that involves a lot of drinking. Whenever I have to do anything tough or new.'

'Like what?'

'Like the first time I went off to do a lecture at Berkeley and I was terrified. Like coming out here to see you and tell you how I feel.'

Emma rose abruptly from the kitchen table and went to the refrigerator to refill her glass. She did not feel ready for this conversation although she'd anticipated it for months.

Alberta watched Emma's back, feeling a rush of tenderness and desire. She sensed Emma's anxiety and it mirrored hers which had hung over her life since last summer. But even stronger than her fear was the certainty that she loved this woman, a realization that only became certain when she spotted Emma running toward her at the airport. Her strong, athletic sprint, the way her curls flew around her face and the pale eyes which shone with joy, wiped out any doubts she had and promised a future worth struggling for.

'I have to make a confession which I guess will say it all,' Alberta said, then watched Emma's face as she returned to the table. The girl could not hide hopeful anticipation. So Alberta continued quickly.

'I am not on my way to Stanford to do a lecture. I was lying about that because I was afraid to just invite myself here to see you. I thought it'd be easier, more casual if it were just a stop on the way somewhere. Then neither of us would have to act like it was a big deal. I just wanted to see you ...'

Alberta stopped when she saw Emma trying to restrain laughter. Then it burst into the room around them. Emma doubled over in raucous laughter that at first frightened Alberta into thinking she'd been completely wrong about how Emma felt.

'You have to stop. Wait ... wait.' Emma said between gulps, trying to regain her composure.

'I have to tell you about this winter. When I came to Boston to see you. I don't have any friends in Cambridge. I just came for you. So I got a room in a hotel and pretended to be going somewhere so you wouldn't think I was forcing myself on you.'

After the laughter stopped, Emma pulled Alberta by her arm up to her room. Alberta had imagined what it would look like all through the winter, but was never able to imagine herself here. Now that she was, it felt natural, inevitable. Emma pulled Alberta's sweater over her head and laid it neatly on the back of a chair. She hurriedly unhooked the white lace bra which contrasted with Alberta's bronze skin. Her mouth found the nipples of Alberta's breasts eagerly, moving quickly from one to the other as she leaned hungrily into them. She pushed Alberta back onto the bed without removing any other clothes. She felt desire rushing over both of them, like a tide come in, suddenly, leaving them breathless. She filled her mouth with Alberta's breast and searched eagerly for the hem of her skirt. She pulled it up to her waist so that little remained between the solid motion of their hips pushing forward to feel each other's desire. Alberta moaned with pleasure at the feel of Emma's hard denim against her naked thighs. She opened her legs to push her cunt against Emma's leg. Dampness flowed through her panties wetting Emma's pant leg as Alberta drove hard to feel herself open for her. Emma's hand slipped inside of her, easily, as it had done that first night downstairs in the den.

Emma pulled herself up to Alberta's face, kissing her mouth and hair and whispered in her ear, 'How much time do we have?'

'Days, years, whatever you want, baby.'

Emma pushed inside of Alberta, feeling her own breath quicken with Alberta's rising passion. She pushed deeper inside, letting her fingers take this woman she needed so much. She felt herself coming simply from the pressure of desire that bore down on them. Still she pushed on, moving over Alberta's clit, and back, deep inside of her, moving her hand in a syncopated rhythm back and forth until Alberta could hold on no longer. Her voice rose from its soft entreaty to a sweet scream of pleasure, the word 'yes' repeated, over and over, until she could speak no more.

They made love to each other through the afternoon and into the night. They finally drifted into sleep holding one another, listening to each other's dreams. When Alberta opened her eyes she found Emma leaning up on her elbow watching her. She smiled with languorous joy.

'It's almost ten o'clock. Maybe I should offer you some dinner?'

'Sounds good. May I use the telephone first?'

'Sure,' Emma said, slightly puzzled. She pulled the phone up from the floor and sat it on the bed. She started to rise and move away but Alberta held on to her leg, not letting her go. With the other hand she punched the buttons briskly.

'Hi, Marsha, it's me. Yeah, yeah I'm here. Listen I want to make a dinner date. I'm cooking. Just a minute.'

Alberta turned to Emma,

'So when can you get to Boston next?'

She turned back to the phone, 'How about Saturday, June

18th, 7 pm?' Alberta giggled low into the phone. The sound made Emma eager to pull Alberta's mouth onto hers again.

'You can bring the wine. We prefer white and none of that cheap shit you got to water down to make it stay down. Alright sister, see ya.'

'Would I be a rude host if I suggest skipping dinner, I'll provide a few snacks and offer to make the best breakfast you've ever had?'

'I was about to suggest that myself. I don't plan to leave this room for twelve hours.' Alberta said and Emma pulled her into her arms.

'At least another twelve hours,' they said in unison.

SEXUAL PREFERENCE

CHERYL CLARKE

I'm a queer lesbian.
Please don't go down on me yet.
I do not prefer cunnilingus.
(There's room for me in the movement.)

Your tongue does not have to prove its prowess
there
to me
now
or even on the first night.

Your mouth all over my body
then there.

NOTES ON AIDS AND SAFER SEX

In the age of AIDS safer sex is an issue relevant to all sexually active lesbians whether or not we perceive ourselves 'at risk' or not. In fact, the discussion is relevant to all lesbians because it is about much more than safer sex techniques.

Although there are arguments about what causes AIDS which may not be resolved for many years, the dominant belief is that a virus called HIV (human immunodeficiency virus) is the main culprit. If someone is infected with this slow acting virus it might remain latent for as long as ten years. During that time the virus can still be passed on to others through the exchange of body fluids containing HIV from one person to another — most commonly semen or blood. However a very small number of lesbians appear to have been infected through woman to woman sexual contact.

At this point in history, and for a whole series of historical reasons, much of what we think of as sex between women appears to have a relatively low risk of transmitting HIV if one of the women is HIV positive. We are referring specifically to sex in which cervical and vaginal secretions are exchanged either through oral sex, or by hand, or sex toy. So far, and we emphasize *so far*, this does not seem to be a high risk activity between women in regards to HIV. Bear in mind that similar exchanges of infected menstrual blood are believed to be much more risky.

Why then should lesbians take on board a discussion of safer sex? We think it's important to consider the context in which we think about AIDS and definitions of lesbianism. If we say that lesbians are at 'low risk', what are we implying about the small but increasing numbers of lesbians who already are HIV positive, and the fact that the majority of them have been infected by sharing unclean needles, from having unprotected sex with HIV positive men, or from using semen for donor insemination from men who have then discovered they are HIV positive? If we declare lesbians a disease free zone what are we saying about these women and what are we saying about lesbianism?

We do not believe that lesbian sex is under special protection from the 'goddess': we *could* be vulnerable to some as yet undetected or imagined new and slow acting virus or even a changed form of HIV. We are vulnerable to other existing STDs (sexually transmitted diseases) which although they may not be life threatening can be a serious drain on our health. Learning about safer sex is a way of collectively talking about what we do sexually.It is also a way of confronting the notion that if you decide to practice safer sex you are 'unclean' or suspect your partner of being so. For all of us, and particularly for marginalized and oppressed groups of people, staying healthy can be an affirming act of resistance.

We are *not* suggesting that every single lesbian in the world should immediately assume she should practice safer sex from this moment on. We are suggesting that it is important both politically and practically to begin to take on board the issue and learn about AIDS and safer sex. Evaluation of 'risk' can only be done effectively when we negotiate new and old sexual relationships in an open and informed way.

An American pamphlet for women puts it this way: 'There are two safer sex issues for women when having sex with women. The first is to determine whether you or your partner are at risk for HIV infection. The second is to decide what, if any, safer sex techniques you should be using. If you are not sure of your risk, play it safe and practise safer sex. Lesbian and bisexual women need to learn to talk about their sex lives, past and present, and negotiate safer sex.'

The authors go on to define safer sex: 'Safer sex with women includes protection from infected blood (including menstrual blood) and from infected cervical and vaginal secretions. Unless you are sure your partner is not HIV positive, you should not go down on her during her period, or immediately before or after. Oral sex at other times may be less risky, but is probably not entirely safe if your partner has an HIV infection.'[1]

Bascially you do not want the possibility of infected blood of any kind to enter your body, or if yours is infected, to enter your partner's — through cuts or abrasions in the mouth, on the hands, in the vagina or genital area, in the arse, or through the eyes.

Do not have oral sex during menstruation with a partner who may be at risk or is HIV positive.

Use latex gloves to protect your hands, particularly when your partner is menstruating, or if doing oral sex, consider using latex squares which cover the genitals.

Sex which includes tying up or whipping is not necessarily unsafe unless it draws blood.

If you are using sex toys (vibrators, dildoes) do not pass them between each other without washing carefully with very hot water and soap or use a solution of household bleach (1 part bleach to 9 parts water is sufficient and be sure to rinse absolutely clean). Even better is to use condoms on sex toys and discard after use on one person. If using a lubricant, try one which contains Nonoxynol-9. There is evidence that it kills HIV but as it may cause irritation in some women, test out on your wrist

201

first. Obviously you should never go directly from your partner's vagina to her arse or vice versa, or her mouth without changing the condom or cleaning the toy.

'Vaginal fluid and faeces in the mouth or through cuts may have caused a small number of transmissions. Urine and saliva are theoretical possibilities, but no cases are definitely attributed to them. Sweat and tears are safe and not even remote possibilities.'[2]

One lesbian active in AIDS education work in the USA defines safer sex as being a series of ongoing processes:
— Obtaining access to up-to-date medical and scientific information
— Starting the process of talking to partners about sex — what we want and don't want, what we fantasize about and what we are afraid of
— Creating a collective atmosphere in which lesbian sexuality can be discussed non-judgementally and politically.[3]

This is not a book about AIDS and safer sex. There are books, pamphlets and organizations which can offer you much more in depth information. We list some of those below.

Where can you get latex or surgical gloves and latex squares or dental dams?

These are accessories we are not used to seeing, let alone using. Where can you find them? Latex gloves are the easiest to obtain. Medical suppliers, like John Bell and Croyden, in London are a good source. Some sex shops like Expectations in London, carry a range of latex gloves. Although the shop is used primarily by men and heterosexual women, there is no reason why lesbians shouldn't go there.

If you are outside London look in your local business telephone book for medical suppliers or call call your local AIDS Line for information on where to obtain latex gloves. Dental dams are harder to come by.

Thrilling Bits, the women's mail order company sell latex gloves and imported dental dams. They claim that so far the British variety are not half as nice to use. Since prices change you will have to write off for their catalogue which costs £2. Then with the catalogue you will receive a voucher which will partially refund the £2 when you make your first order.

Some lesbians in the USA are cutting up condoms to use as squares — unroll, cut lengthwise and stretch out into a flat piece of material.

John Bell and Croyden, 54 Wigmore Street, London W1
Expectations, 75 Great Eastern Street, London EC2. Tel: 01 739 0292
Thrilling Bits, BCMBITS, London WC1N 3XX

References

1. *MAKING IT A Woman's Guide to Sex in the Age of AIDS.*
   Cindy Patton and Janis Kelly, Firebrand Sparks Pamphlet £2
   Firebrand Books 1987

2. ibid

3. Cindy Patton in an unpublished paper 1988. Thanks to the author.

Books

Women and AIDS Crisis, Diane Richardson
Pandora

AIDS: The Women Edited by Ines Rieder and Patricia Ruppelt
Cleis Press.

Organisations

The Terrence Higgins Trust, BM AIDS, London WC1N 3XX
Helpline: 01 242 1010

Lesbian Line: London 01 251 6911. And see Helplines in The Pink Paper for out of
London lines.

Positively Women (An autonomous group for all women who are HIV positive)
Get in touch through: THEnterprises, 333 Grays Inn Road, WC1X 8PX. 01 837 9705

Black Lesbian and Gay Centre, BM 4390, London WC1N 3XX. 01 885 3543

THE SHEBA COLLECTIVE

Michelle McKenzie has been working at Sheba for the past two years. She is an active member of the Black Lesbian and Gay Centre Project. In the past she has been a grad, a custom framer, translator, researcher, shop assistant, cleaner. She is currently an aspiring artist and writer. A firm believer in the power of the word, she has a reputation for hanging on in there against the odds.

Araba Yacoba Mercer has always wanted to work with books and thanks her lucky stars that she found a niche at Sheba, almost three years ago. She writes occasional reviews, is co-founder of *Quim*, the first UK lesbian sex magazine, and is active in Black lesbian and gay politics. She lives in graffiti-stained south London with her lover, DMT.

Sue O'Sullivan has worked at Sheba for three and a half years, arriving there after five years working on *Spare Rib Magazine*. She freelances as an editor and occasional journalist and is a member of the *Feminist Review* collective. Currently she is working with the group Positively Women on a book for Sheba by women who are HIV positive, and also on a book about women and anal health problems called *The Bottom Line* for Camden Press. She does the pools regularly, demonstrating that even sensible older girls have impossible dreams.

RaeAnn Robertson came to London from Western Canada in 1982 and has been working at Sheba for almost four years. Her main loves in life are finance work, computers and her sweetheart, Cris, but not necessarily in that order.

CONTRIBUTORS' BIOGRAPHIES

Tina Bays
Tina Bays is a lesbian pushing fifty who used to be nervous about the menopause and isn't anymore. She's also a feminist who takes the long view and still believes in Revolution with a big 'R'.

Diane Biondo
Diane Biondo is the author of four plays, *Slipstreaming, Hitting Home, Penance,* and *Four Walls.* She has co-written a chapter for *Feminism and Censorship: The Current Debate* (Prism Press, 1988). Her short story, 'Something to Cry About', appears in the anthology of crime stories *Reader, I Murdered Him* (The Women's Press, 1988). Since first coming to London from Brooklyn, New York in 1981, she has earned her living working in the book trade.

Ruth Bowen
Ruth Bowen is thirty-five and lives alone in North-East London. In 1983 she joined a lesbian writing group and, when that ceased to meet, established another in 1987. She has completed a novel and continues to write poetry.

Cheryl Clarke
Cheryl Clarke is a Black lesbian poet and the author of two books of poetry: *Narratives: Poems in the Tradition of Black Women* (1982) and *Living As A Lesbian* (Firebrand Books 1986). She has completed a new volume of poetry, *Humid Pitch,* to be published late 1989. She has been a member of *Conditions* editorial collective since 1981.

Fiona Cooper
I live and work in London, dreaming of The Hanging Gardens of Babylon, or is it the Floating Gardens of Mexico? or Cocktails at sunset and breakers

on the shore? My work has been described as 'ineradicably Mills and Boon', and I've had short stories in *Cosmopolitan* (UK), *Woman's Day* (Australia), and *Passion Fruit* (Pandora Press). I've freelanced as ineradicable drag-hag for the gay press. My first novel, *Rotary Spokes*, a comic lesbian odyssey, was published by Brilliance Books in 1988, and the second, *Heartbreak on the High Sierra*, will be published by Virago in 1989.

Mandy Dee (8/8/52 — 31/10/88)
I am white, born working class, lesbian feminist, with anarchist tendencies. I am bedbound with Multiple Sclerosis, but it is essential for everyone to remember and never to forget that I was born spastic and I was brought up as a disabled child, so in my mid-twenties I began to be an adult disabled from birth who also had a progressive disease. There are not many women in England with that experience. When I write anything it is a race between ability and exhaustion to get it down before I become too physically tired to think or write. I live in South London and have fought rivers of blood to get the house I now have. The situation for disabled housing is desparate. I dream constantly about the special showcase school for the disabled I went to. The experiences that we all had as disabled people and disabled children keeps me alive now.

Fifi
Born in the bosom of sweet Africa she now lives in inner-city London. She dreams of the day when all people will be free to live and love, night or day, without fear of the clock running out of time. She writes in the still of the night, alone.

Berta R Freistadt
Berta R Freistadt is a Londoner. She has had poetry and short stories published in several magazines and feminist anthologies. She is also a playwright. She is slightly bemused at being in this book as her life leaves her little time to be erotic. But she is taking lessons from the cat.

Jewelle Gomez
Jewelle Gomez is the author of *Flamingoes and Bears*, a collection of poetry and a forthcoming lesbian vampire novel. She has reviewed books for *Belle Lettres*, *The New York Times*, and *New Directions for Women*.

Caroline Halliday
Caroline Halliday is a white lesbian, born in 1947 in London. She works as a freelance consultant on management training courses, and teaches lesbian creative writing. Her poetry has appeared in a number of anthologies, including *Naming the Waves* (1988), *The New British Poetry* (1988), and in her own collection, *Some Truth, Some Change* (1983). She combines writing with

being a co-parent, her daughter lives with her half the week. She writes novels as well as poetry, and the present work comes from an experimental novel called *Where the River Goes*, which is looking for a publisher!

Bernadette Halpin

Bernadette Halpin: Leo; thirty-four; has lived for seven years in inner-city lesbian nation (aka Hackney), passing her summers with the Hackney Raiders Softball team, mostly admiring women from the outfield who have something called co-ordination; thinks humour is preferably the greatest turn-on.

Amanda Hayman

Amanda Hayman is thirty-seven, a fat, white, middle class Lesbian Separatist who has lived in Japan for eight years. She teaches English in Tokyo, whilst reserving the greater part of her energy for the Lesbian community there, and her writing. Her first piece of fiction, *Wishful Thinking*, appears in an anthology of lesbian bedtime stories (Tough Dove Books), she has also had her work published in *The Coming Out Stories*, second edition, (Crossing Press). Over the past five years, Amanda has had several articles on lesbian/feminist theory published in the USA and the UK. She loves cats, Linda, The Archers, and being a lesbian.

Maria Jastrzebska

Maria Jastrzebska was born in Warsaw, Poland, and came to England as a child. Her poems have recently appeared in *Naming The Waves* (Virago), *Forum Palek — The Polish Women's Forum*, and *The New British Poetry 1968-88* (Paladin). Generally a serious poet, well-wrapped in woolly scarf and layers, she has been known to flirt outrageously.

Terri L Jewell

Terri Lynn Jewell, born October 4, 1954, Louisville, Kentucky, USA. Came out as a dyke in 1976 and as a writer in 1981. My poetry, essays and book reviews have appeared in over 200 different literaries and magazines, most being lesbian. There is nothing more erotic than a fat lesbian who shows that everything in life belongs to her.

Esther Y Kahn

Esther Y Kahn was born May 1956, the love-child of a rebellious jewish woman who later committed suicide. Esther was adopted from a jewish orphanage by a working/middle class Hungarian/Russian couple who were soon divorced, and Esther grew up in cosmopolitan central London with her mother and brother Max. She is currently a film-maker, poet, DJ and youth worker. She is involved in Esther Kahn's Jewish Dance Palace and other jewish cultural ventures. Her favourite breakfast is coffee and cigarettes and her favourite colour is gold. In her spare time Esther likes to recreate her grandmother's favourite hungarian/jewish recipes. She also likes dancing, drinking and cinema. She has no children, no cats.

L A Levy

Born in London 1963 into a family of Persian and European Jews. L A Levy writes, paints, works in institutions and does political work in this country against the Israeli occupation. This is her first published work. She recognises that some readers will be unfamiliar with some of the language she uses and asks that these people create dialogue and their own research.

Pearlie McNeill

I have to tell you, this is truly a first for me. I've been writing with determined intent since 1975 but serious pleasure writing? What a delicious habit. Like masturbation and lesbianism, erotic writing is something we are *not* encouraged to do. I approached the challenge with the same hot stubborness I experienced, aged five, when my Mum caught me doing what she called 'jibblajerks'. I'm fifty this year and still going strong. Hope you are too.

Mindy Meleyal

I was born in Hull in 1951 and I am a school teacher. I started writing four years ago and for the last two and a half years I have been encouraged by the Northern Dyke Writers Group of which I am a member. I live alone, I have no children and I am a cancer survivor (five years plus). I am also white and a Leo. This is my first published work.

Cuntessa de Mons Veneris

The Cuntessa is descended from the Ashanti people, and has come to Britain via the West Indies. She feels she has only succeeded in writing erotic stories if lesbians get turned on by them.

Nina Rapi

Nina Rapi was born in Argos Orestiko, Greece. She writes poems, short stories and plays; some published and/or performed, others not yet. She lives in south London.

Barbara Smith

Barbara Smith learned to write when she was five, had her first sexual experience when she was seven, and learned the violin when she was eight. Having thus acquired the necessary prerequisites and accomplished the co-ordination of left and right hands she then turned to writing erotic short stories, some of which have since appeared in *Square Peg* and *Gay Scotland*.

Cherry Smyth

Cherry Smyth was born in Northern Ireland and came to London in 1982. She has lectured and written articles and reviews on lesbians in film for *Square Peg*, *Spare Rib*, and *The Pink Paper*. She frequently reads her poetry with the Irish Womens' Writing Network. She fears cultural assimilation and sees writing as a way of preserving her Irish identity and affirming her lesbianism.

Liann Snow

In youth: obsessive; angrily optimistic; indignantly homosexual; determinedly communicative of my own experience (through painting, poems, songs and prose). Now: a graduate; bemusedly lesbian. I write and draw but train to be a gardener. I also paint the Great Goddess (determinedly communicative of that experience).

Caroline Trusty

I was born in London, 1965. I am a lesbian feminist keen on pursuing Green and Anarchist politics as a lifestyle. I want to travel the world on my bicycle, Sheila. At the moment I am in Australia. This is the first time I have been published, but my aspirations are to write much more, so hopefully it won't be the last.

Storme Webber

Storme Webber was born in 1959 in Seattle, Washington. She is a poet, singer, visual artist currently performing with the Stations Theatre Collective in New York City. She has performed/exhibited extensively in San Fransisco and New York: including Ntozake Shange's *3 views of mt. fuji*; *life on the water*; *galeria de la raza C.U.A.N.D.O.*. She is the author of *diasporal poetry and graphics*.

for liberation through creation
insistence on resistance
we honor our ancestors
we make our children proud
FREEDOM IS COMING